TIED TO HIM: MY BFF

TIED TO HIM: MY BFF

BWWM EROTICA COLLECTION

ROWENA

ISBN: 979-8745346149

First Electronic Edition: March 2015

First Paperback Edition: April 2021

CONTENTS

CAPTURED BY YOU

POSSESSED BY YOU

CLAIMED BY YOU

CAPTURED BY YOU

No man has been able to capture young, ebony hottie Gina's imagination the way her hunky, blue-eyed military best friend, Jake, has.

Jake hasn't had a chance to lock down a long-term relationship himself, but he's had plenty of time to think about his beautiful brown-skinned buddy and what he wants to do to her while he's away at war.

Neither thinks the other sees them as more than a friend, but this time, as Jake heads home from deployment, he plans to show Gina not only how much he has missed her, but how much more than a friend she's about to become!

1

———

JAKE

I spot Gina before she spots me, even though I'm the most conspicuous one of the two of us in my military uniform and with my pale skin and light blue eyes among the diverse airport crowd.

Gina blends in more with the multicolored mass of people. She's sort of the opposite of me: dark hair, dark eyes, dark skin.

I'm a head above the crowd at six-two, which probably helps my vantage point while Gina's a mere five-four, but I'd also been looking for her long before she could be seen.

To be honest, I'd know Gina's form and that pretty brown face of hers anywhere, and while I know that as soon as her eyes turn my way she'll register me immediately too, it's like she's a magnet to me; I knew where she'd be standing long before I actually spotted her.

The joy on her face when she sees me a mere few seconds after I spot her (although it feels longer), warms me throughout; the sight of her smile always does.

We hurry to each other and I put down my duffel bag to prepare for grabbing her in a hug, anticipating the second she reaches me and throws her warm, slender body against mine.

I love moments like this when I get to hold her this tight for this long and she doesn't suspect a thing, but why would she suspect I'm getting more out of our hug than the usual friendly human touch after making it home from a war zone?

I bet she has no clue how much I enjoy the feel of her soft breasts against my chest, my arms around her slim, shapely form, and the reminder of her narrow waistline.

I love that I can rest my head on top of hers and get a whiff of whatever shampoo or hair oil she used last—all the familiar sounds, smells, and feel of her.

While I'm grateful and happy to see this old friend of mine again, I have something else besides catching up in store for her.

I gently kiss her cheek.

As I feel myself grow hard, I pull away from her.

I'm not sure if she noticed the change.

Her face indicates she hasn't; in fact, I can practically see her transformation to a familiar personality as she begins to get all buddy-buddy and reintroduce our way of interacting with a tasteless joke.

"Still couldn't manage to tan, huh?" she says with that disarming, radiant smile of hers, and I force out a slight chuckle in response.

Once in a while, she finds some way to make fun of my pasty skin, and I sort of want to make her pay for that too since I can't make fun of her the same way without risking her getting offended.

Instead, I just take it and I poke at her in other ways, carrying on our friendship as if the thought of fucking her has never occurred to me.

But it sure as hell has.

I've wanted to strip her naked for a while—to take in her body in all its nude glory and see what her tits look like beneath those plain-ass T-shirts she wears around me in our casual, platonic comfort. I want to get an eyeful of her slit before pushing myself inside of her, feel her slick walls squeezing me as I pound her flesh, owning her body at last.

I'm sure she still feels completely safe around me, but she shouldn't.

I have a burning desire to show her how unsafe she is. Scare her a little. To see her eyes widen a bit in fear as she realizes she is entirely at my mercy.

I would never hurt her—not in any way that would actually bring her pain—but I want to remind her she's a woman and I'm a man, and there are certain things that women and men do together.

I don't want her to continue taking my mercy on her for granted. To be honest, I'm in a game-playing mood—I'm down for a little cat and mouse.

Besides, my cock throbs at the thought of her more frequently than before, and I have pretty much lost my patience.

She'd probably run screaming in the opposite direction if she knew what I was thinking, and the thought of that makes me smile more.

Gina has never looked at me *that way*, although I've seen her eyes appreciate my fit physique.

She's still sort of safe for now—I have a lot of horror to purge from my brain, and although I'll never get rid of it all, it'll be a few days before I can clear the post-war fog and act fairly normal again.

"Dude, you know I'm here; just call me when you're ready," Gina says as she pulls up to my condo. About twenty minutes have passed since we left the airport. "We'll do sushi or something—go for drinks, karaoke, whatever. Just give me a shout."

Where the hell does she think she's going? Why is she taking off?

"I know you have to shower and purge, etc.," she says as if she read my mind.

She's right, of course, and there's no reason for me to get offended or take her leaving right away personally, but I would have liked a little more time with her before she took off for home—I don't like when she denies me anything, especially her time.

Does she have no idea how much she keeps me grounded, sane? Does she have no clue how much I need her at this part of my transition? How can she leave me when I need her most?

Thinking about coming back to her gets me through my deployment, and once back, thinking about ways to monopolize her time keeps me going.

I remind myself that, just as she said, whenever I call her to me she'll come, and that could easily be later tonight.

Though she's taking off now, I know I'll see her again soon, and I look forward to it with more than my usual enthusiasm.

I have a big surprise for her, and if I make it back from my next deployment (whenever that comes), she won't greet me at the airport alone.

But everything in due time.

I will find my way inside of her soon enough, and she has no idea what's coming.

I don't know how or when, but before I leave this place again, Gina will be mine.

2

——

GINA

When Jake asked me to get him from the airport, how could I say no? We've been good friends since high school, and even though an airport run isn't exactly convenient, it doesn't matter when you're doing it for a friend like Jake.

He probably asked me because I have such a flexible schedule too—with him flying in on a Wednesday, I'm guessing most other people he knows have to work and save a day off for something more urgent.

Besides, airport pickups are so tricky; they can take fifteen minutes or an hour—not exactly something you want to bet your lunch time on.

Luckily, I have a job where I choose my hours, so I'm pretty much available anytime. I would hate to think of Jake having to sort out such a simple luxury by himself after all he must have gone through abroad.

How could he not want to be welcomed back into the country by a familiar face and just relax in the passenger's seat on the way to a home he hasn't seen in over a year?

I like my part in easing him back into regular society—I get to greet him pretty much as soon as he arrives and eventually catch him up on what's been going on in his absence.

I don't want to hear about what he's had to do abroad unless he wants to share, which he usually doesn't—he takes the time we spend together to temporarily forget.

Catching him up on everything usually doesn't take very long, and once that's done, we still have more we can do—besides knowing each other since junior high, we have a lot of things in common, so we can actually hang out and have fun together like any set of regular, platonic friends.

We found out we had gaming in common kind of randomly—Street Fighter, in particular.

In ninth grade, while walking down the school hallway, he overheard me bragging about beating the latest game with a character I don't usually use, and we chatted from there about that particular game, and then moved on to other fighting games.

Then, of course, we started challenging each other, and I think he underestimated me as a girl, but I beat his ass pretty mercilessly at first.

It made him improve, and we went back and forth

kicking each other's ass in our living rooms and in arcades.

Since then, we have graduated to interacting with each other in other ways.

Back in the day, we pretty much kept our interactions to gaming sessions, but once we got close, we started chatting about other stuff, including relationships with other people.

Once we got to the age where hanging out with each other became awkward for significant others, we learned to keep our distance while keeping close through gaming apps—online games.

The times we were both single, we saw movies together or met for lunch, and we carried on like our separation during our relationship-of-the-moment didn't happen.

Through it all, we remained close, and these days, we still challenge each other to fighting games, but we mostly take it easy and do TV show marathons.

Jake hasn't had a real girlfriend in a while—he hasn't found one happy to be committed to him while he's away for long periods of time and may or not come back, so as far as I know, he now only indulges in meaningless flings, temporarily giving up on having a steady partner.

As for me, I continue to date and have found myself in a string of relationships that last anywhere from a few weeks to a few months. Actually, I haven't been in a long-term relationship in a while myself.

Honestly, I find Jake incredibly sexy. I've probably been subconsciously making myself available every time I expect him back because I look forward to having his blue eyes on me, even though I know I'm not his type and he's not looking at me like that. He has only gone after brunettes of the fair-complexioned variety; I've never even seen him look at a brown-skinned girl, except for obvious super beautiful celebrity types that everyone can't help but stare at.

Me, I'm all right—a solid seven at least. But most people probably think that, right?

I know I'm like a little sister to him, and I use all my acting skills to pretend I see him like that too, but I can't help feeling sexually attracted to him—he is fit and strong in a way that makes him oh so fine.

This wasn't always the case—Jake was kind of awkward-looking in high school with his super pale skin dotted with pimples, and he was sort of scrawny to boot.

The process of growing up eventually got rid of the acne, and military training changed his body.

Now he exudes alpha, and the insecure eyes of his youth have settled into a more confident but almost empty look of a jaded man. Being thrust into the face of the worst of humanity has to change you in ways.

Somehow, that steady, unreadable look of his makes him even more sexy.

I can tell he tries to shake himself into normalcy as quickly as possible for my benefit. He tries to act like he used to before his first deployment, and he succeeds for the most part, but I know he struggles mentally and otherwise with his violent line of work.

Things must look so ridiculous to him when he returns—he practically goes from holding dying fellow soldiers screaming out for their mother right before they pass, to watching people yap about a Kardashian. What a bizarre existence, going from one world to another like that.

I'm just glad he hasn't pushed me away in some overall withdrawal from mankind—I've heard of that happening to soldiers like him.

I try not to be frivolous around him unless he encourages it, because who knows? Maybe every now and then, shooting the breeze about silly shit is a welcome shot at normal for him.

Whatever. I sort of let him lead the way.

In the meantime, I try to keep my attraction to him far away from our interactions. I bury it as deep as it can go because I value our friendship tremendously, and if we change it in any way, I might lose him.

Plus, to be honest, he's one of those men that I feel in danger of losing my mind about—like I'd feel tied to him in a way that isn't usually the case if he ever had his way with me.

I'm far more vulnerable to him than is good for me —a guy like him could break my heart.

He has a dominating aura, and it makes me feel

submissive and suggestive to his will, and as a result, it leaves me open.

Most guys I date can't get close to reaching me and making me care, but Jake—Jake has always been close, and he's the only guy I know with the ability to get even closer.

My heart's in my throat practically the whole time he's away, and when I know he's coming home, nothing takes me higher than the thought of that—except for actually seeing him. Then even that's surpassed by the moment we touch, and his muscular arms wrap around my body, squeezing me in an affectionate hold.

I love the feeling of being pressed against his firm chest.

That's as far as we usually go, whether it's hello or goodbye—we don't do the kiss-on-the-cheek thing like a lot of friends and family do.

Today, however, as we embraced among the airport crowd, his lips met my cheek before we pulled away.

I felt the tingle of contact long after we drove off, and at the moment, I didn't return the gesture—I was too busy trying to hide all signs of the joy that brief kiss brought me.

Considering our bond, that minor action shouldn't be a big deal—it was simply an expression of affection and appreciation like any other.

But honestly, I sense something different about him this time, and it scares me a little.

I've never been afraid of him before, and I have

always respected the path he took and the way he puts his life on the line on behalf of our country. Despite knowing he's a soldier who probably has at least a few deaths under his belt, I've never felt in danger when around him—violence is reserved for whomever the government has declared the enemy and sent him after.

But the moment his lips met my cheek, my spidey sense started tingling.

I feel kind of stupid because how could he possibly be a danger to me?

Maybe if he finally has some sort of psychotic break, loses it and snaps my neck in some sort of PTSD reaction or something, but I'm not worried about that.

He might not be completely stable as a result of his experiences, but my gut insists it's not my *life* that's in danger around him.

3

JAKE

I try to ignore the way my heart drops when Gina's car is finally out of sight, then I turn my attention to my condo.

Since I'm out of town for such long periods, I rent it out, and luckily, I have a dependable, trustworthy friend who helps me take care of the details and acts as a bridge between me and the temporary tenant: Gina.

Gina eases tenants in and out and takes care of details relating to deposits and cleanup. Of course, I pay her a fraction of the rental payments for sort of acting as a landlord on my behalf.

So far, over three years and four tenants, nothing major has been broken or stolen, and there's been only one fight over a deposit.

We're pretty careful about who we let stay here, and I'm relieved to see my place has no signs of having been trashed in my absence yet again.

Sure, Gina would have told me if a paint job was needed or about missing or broken items, but it looks like everything went smoothly, and Gina has had someone come in and do a thorough cleaning, which I send her money to do—I like the place to not only look neat and spotless but smell like a Pine Sol flood passed through.

I drop my bag in my bedroom and continue to inspect the place. I'm more than pleased with what I see.

I don't know what I'd do without her; Gina is truly a gem.

Satisfied, I take a long, hot shower and work on just blanking my mind, concentrating on how good it feels to have the spray on my skin.

I'm going to arrange a full body massage, then call around and make plans to see various friends so I can start acting like a normal human again—hit up some bars, eat pizza, watch a crappy movie. Pretend like I care about so-and-so's new job or baby. And once I've got all of that rolling, I'll do what I long to do most: contact Gina and arrange to see her again as soon as possible.

I'll leave her alone for the rest of today and maybe even tomorrow, if I can stand it.

I wake up from a nightmare and immediately look to my side as if expecting to see Gina in bed next to me.

I wish she was so I could hold her and ease myself back into sleep.

I have to stop myself from dialing her so I can hear her voice, even if just to say (annoyed), "What are you —crazy? It's four a.m.!"

I'm not sure if she'd actually say that—she'd probably get concerned and think something's wrong, that she needs to help me.

"What do you need?" she's more likely to say. "I'll be right over."

It's too easy, really—she'll willingly walk into any trap I set for her.

She has no reason to suspect I'd be up to no good, and she cares so much for me, she'd want to make sure I have what I need—even if it's just an ear in the middle of the night.

She has that look in her eyes sometimes that I see in other people's eyes—awkward sympathy about my line of work. Most people don't really think about what I actually go through and sort of dutifully (and emptily) thank me for my service.

Anyway, I could probably call Gina right now and not piss her off, but I don't want to do that to her—she deserves at least one more night of obliviously thinking of me as just an old friend, wrapped in the comfort of knowing she's been living life on her own terms before I impose my plans on her.

When my eyes open again and I realize it's morning, I know I can't wait another day to see Gina.

Torture returned to me in my next set of dreams, but those times, torture came in the form of her.

I can't take it any longer—I must have her body against mine; I must claim Gina once and for all.

I know she likes to sleep in sometimes, so I wait until after ten a.m. to call her.

"What are you up to today?" I ask as she answers.

"I didn't make any solid plans since I know you'll want me to squeeze you in here and there over the next week or so."

I have to stifle a laugh because she has no idea how right she is, how literal those words will become.

My cock is already twitching in anticipation.

"Come on down, then! We'll figure out something. I owe you lunch, at least, for looking after my place."

"You know I can't resist free food! Okay, I'll head over in about an hour; I'm not hungry right now, but you can feed me later. In the meantime, I want to show you this new Netflix series..."

I let her blab on while I savor the emotions churning in me, steadily increasing in power: affection, joy, and desire—all aimed at Gina, like my cock will soon be.

It's thickening now as I think about the chance I'll soon have to push it between her boobs, to have her luscious mouth close over it, her warm tongue slithering over my shaft.

I think about the relief I'll feel once I finally slide my cock into her and start pushing against the sweet pussy lips I've only dreamt of.

My cock grows painfully harder as I imagine her moaning in my ear, my body pressing against hers while she holds on to me in the most intimate hug, my dick exploring the tight, warm cavern of her body as I bring us both to the ultimate pleasure.

Finally, I will shoot my seed into her, squirting my cum at her uterus in hopes that I take root in her, my fertilizing fluid following its natural course and leaving a part of me behind to grow inside of her over the next several months.

I will take Gina again and again until I'm sure she's full of my seed and bound to me in more ways than one.

My dear friend is doomed.

4
___

GINA

I am far too excited when I receive Jake's call to come over.

This must be what people in real romantic relationships feel, and I can see why people are addicted to the whole thing; it makes you feel alive.

I haven't felt this kind of emotional dependence and excitement for a person outside of my friendship with Jake, and I long to feel that type of passion with the person I'm dating or in an actual relationship with. But I also like my individual freedom, and not having to worry about how my actions will affect anyone but myself, so I find it fairly easy to keep an emotional distance.

I like being able to change jobs whenever I want with no real responsibility weighing on me, and I like not having my life determined by emotions connecting me to some other human being.

I like that I won't lose my mind if the guy I'm dating forgets to call, and that none of the dudes I've met so far can talk me into doing something that will probably only benefit him ultimately: moving a few states away on account of his new job or school, or changing some other plan of mine to accommodate him. I've seen way too many chicks rearrange their lives for some dude not even guaranteed to stick around: delaying continuing education or getting rid of friendships—with males and females—as a result of trying to give more to him, and of course, guys never do the same.

Not fucking me.

The only guy who twists my heart when it's been too long since I've heard from him is Jake, and I've learned to control that yearning for the most part.

I like that, because of his periods of physical distance, I'm safe from the potential devastation he could cause if we were anything more than friends.

When I pull up to Jake's place, however, something doesn't feel right, and I get worried.

I know I shouldn't, but I don't want to ignore the feeling either.

I consider texting him that something came up and then taking off, but I immediately feel bad for considering doing that to my old friend—he needs company and wants to hang out as usual, and here I am, thinking about abandoning him at a time he might be most vulnerable.

I shake my head as if I can shake sense into myself that way.

Perhaps the problem is that my heart feels like it's about to be opened to him in a way it hasn't been before—like I'm on the verge of suddenly falling for him. I definitely feel like I'm on the edge of some cliff.

Before I can change my mind and speed out of there, Jake comes outside with a smile and a wave, and there's no way I can turn my back on him now.

I leave the car, wondering why the strange feeling still hasn't left me in the face of his sunshine.

We embrace quickly, then I follow him inside.

"So glad you could make it," he says. "Had a nightmare last night and figured I could use some distractions."

Immediately, my unease lifts.

"Glad I can help," I say with a genuine smile.

"Water? Orange juice?" he offers, heading to the kitchen.

"Carrot juice," I say, knowing it's in his refrigerator because I bought it, along with the other groceries his cupboards and refrigerator are loaded with; I usually take care of that once the cleaning lady's done.

Ever since the first time I bought him a few things so his kitchen wasn't completely empty when he returned, he sends me extra money to cover costs in case I do it again—which I always do. He sends me far more money than I need, so he ends up a little more stocked than that first time.

We shoot the breeze for a bit, and it takes a while, but I eventually notice something: Jake's eyes haven't left me in the past few minutes, and the intensity of his concentrated gaze is starting to disturb me.

I'm reminded of the feeling I had when I first pulled up, then remember even further back to yesterday when he kissed me on the cheek.

I stare back at him for a moment, but he still doesn't break his gaze, and my sense of dread grows.

I feel stalked so I try to shake him off with a snap of my fingers and a light "Hello! Earth to Jake!"

I smile as wide as I can manage.

Jake doesn't smile back or play along with my pretense that everything's still fairly normal.

It is clear that something in the air has changed.

My heart beats even harder against my chest as fear surges through me.

The only man I've ever known with the power to bend me and change the course of my life by having me give in to his will is looking at me with something I didn't expect and wasn't prepared for in the least.

I can no longer pretend to misinterpret the look in Jake's eyes—he looks like an animal about to pounce.

"Why are you looking at me like that?" I finally say softly, though I already know the answer.

Guess I'm still hoping he proves me wrong.

"You know why," he says deeply, still staring me down.

My legs feel like they've turned to jelly.

I try to keep my voice light and steady. "Well, I asked, didn't I? So I guess I *don't* know."

His eyes finally leave my face to travel down my body in a deliberately slow manner, reaching my chest and lingering on my breasts before traveling the rest of the way down.

I suddenly feel like I'm on fire as blood rushes to the surface of every part of me.

His eyes return to my face.

"You still don't know?" he says, his tone calm but full of danger.

"You can't have me," I blurt in an embarrassingly pitiful voice.

I swear I meant it to come out strong and sure, but my gut already knew what time it was, and I'm on the edge of that cliff again.

His mouth quirks a little, a twitch of a tiny, one-sided smile, but it's not a real smile—it's the shell of an imitation never reaching his steady blue eyes.

"You know that's not true, Gina. I *can* have you, and I'm about to."

He stands and heads toward me, clearly about to prove his words true, but... you know how, in dangerous situations, that fight or flight instinct kicks in? Well, without a single thought, I go into flight mode and begin to run.

For some reason, I decide to run toward the back of the condo, instead of trying to exit through the front door.

Maybe some part of me suspected Jake would anticipate that move and beat me there, blocking the door, and my chance to escape him would be gone.

Either way, I disappear through the first door I reach—his bedroom—and lock it quickly behind me.

It seems my unexpected move bought me enough time to lock it right before he reaches me—I beat him by about half a second and lean against the locked door, panting in partial relief.

He slams himself against the door.

"Let me in, Gina," he says, then slams against the door again.

I know the door will give way to his muscular body soon—that hard, strong vessel strengthened further by adrenaline and mad desire.

"I'm calling for help!" I say, then pretend to call, since I left my phone on the living room coffee table.

I hope he doesn't realize it's all a lie.

"Please come quickly—he's lost his mind!" I say.

"I haven't lost my mind," his muffled voice says from behind the door. "I've lost my patience."

He slams against the door again.

I move away from it, preparing for it to give way.

There's nothing else I can do—Jake will be in here with me soon.

I had hoped that pretending to make that call for help would make him think twice and deter him, that knowing someone else had been filled in on what he's up to and is possibly on the way here would calm him down.

But I remember the way his blue eyes burned, the way my instincts kicked into high gear, warning me that my old friend was dangerously aroused and about to pounce.

I had bought little time with the door between us, and as I watch it finally fly open, part of me sinks, despite all the other elevated parts.

I am doomed.

"Hello," Jake says calmly—as if he didn't just break a door open.

I take a step back. "Jake, please…"

"I want you, Gina," he interrupts, taking a few steps forward and closing the distance between us, "and I'm finally going to have you. Do you have any idea how long…?"

It seems he has changed his mind about talking because instead of finishing his sentence, he tears his shirt off.

My eyes get stuck on his defined chest and abs before reminding myself that I need to come up with a plan B fast.

Then I get distracted by his sinewy, masculine beauty again.

"You're not going to get away," he says, "so don't fool yourself. Try to get past me and I'll grab you—you know it. You have nowhere to go, Gina—nowhere but on that bed—and no choice but to take everything I have to give you."

"Please, Jake…"

"I think I will," he says. "I'll do everything I can to please you, Gina, starting with this…"

He drops his pants and I'm pretty sure my eyes actually bulge at the sight of his hard, thick cock saluting me.

"God, I want to savor every moment of this," he says. "Every smell, every taste. Too bad you called in reinforcements."

He has reached me and rips my top off easily.

"Now I'll have to rush, and if you try to resist me once more, I'm going to fuck you so hard you won't soon forget it. I'm going to fuck you hard, anyway—just not as hard as I would if you make me angrier."

He starts undoing my jeans and I fruitlessly try to thwart his efforts, despite his threat.

"Relax," he says as he unclasps, unzips, and then pushes my jeans down.

I'm standing there in my panties and bra and have never felt more vulnerable and helpless in my life.

"I'll take care of you," he says, then pushes me onto the bed.

Before I can recover, he is hovering over me and I am trapped beneath him, enduring his blue gaze on me.

His eyes follow the line of my shoulders, the swell of my breasts, and just as I think he's about to rake his eyes down my torso, his mouth is suddenly on my neck and it makes me arch my back.

My skin is oversensitive, and the feel of soft lips and wet tongue there makes my body tingle furiously.

My center roars to life, and he continues to suckle my neck, switching sides.

"Jake," is all I can say, and it comes out as a whimper.

"Who did you call to come over?" he says between kisses and sucking. "Who do you think can help you?"

"No one," I admit.

He breaks contact with my neck to flash me a wicked grin.

Then his mouth finds the swell of my breasts visible outside of my bra, and he lightly kisses them while he works to unclasp it.

He succeeds, flinging my bra to the side while he bends to enclose the whole of one breast with his mouth, then the other, flicking his tongue over my aching nipples.

My body wants his mouth all over me, but there's no way I'm about to say it; I'm still supposed to be resisting. This is not what we should be doing—we're friends and should keep it that way!

"Jake..."

He stops and raises slightly to pull my panties down, and his eyes take in my middle while he flings my underwear aside.

"Finally," he says, staring. "I've always wondered if

you'd be narrow or meaty there." He raises his eyes to mine. "You're beautiful," he says, then he bends his head to my core and I cry out as his mouth reaches my pussy, the first contact of his lips on mine.

I writhe and grab the sheets as he begins to suck me and flick his tongue over my folds, teasing me here and there with a lick of my clit.

I am completely lost to him.

He eats me like a master, and I can't stop the moans and cries bubbling from me, I can't stop my body's shudders and twists and thrusts toward him, the waves of pleasure taking over me.

When he stops, I am helplessly panting and aching for more, and I don't care if he dips his face back into my fiery center or stuffs me with his dick—I need more stimulation right now.

It's torture to have him just stare at me for the next few seconds, and I know he's enjoying watching my wordless surrender.

"You're so wet," he says in wonder, "and you look so fucking hot, writhing and breathing like that."

Finally, he puts me out of my misery by burying his face between my legs again, and joy and pain collide.

I start fucking his face—I need to bring an end to this growing insanity, this aching need that has taken over me and wiped out all sense and logic, this torturous pleasure running through my body and jerking it in all directions.

"Oh god, Jake," I say as I feel myself getting closer to the edge.

I fuck his face more furiously, grabbing his head with my hands as I press my throbbing parts against him.

He slips a finger inside me and takes his tongue-bathing up a notch, skillfully twisting and flicking the flexible pleasure organ over my feminine folds in coordination with his sliding finger until I reach my peak.

My moans explode in a massive climactic groan, and my body starts another flood.

I lie motionless and panting, unable to look at Jake or process anything but the nirvana clouding me as I slowly float back down to earth.

I can feel my core still pulsing, my heart pounding, my body relaxing in warm gratitude.

I feel sort of drunk in my ecstasy.

After a while, I become completely aware of Jake again, and embarrassment fills me at being so exposed.

More than that, I know the moment I lock eyes with him, he will take my heart—I just don't know if it'll happen before or after he takes my body, as he is clearly poised to do.

5

JAKE

I have never gotten so much pleasure from giving it before.

I find myself thirsty for every change in Gina's face, every sign of her joy. I want to give it to her over and over again, and I have every intention of doing just that, starting right now.

My cock couldn't get any harder, and I'm not sure she could get any wetter.

I only hope I don't cream before I get a good amount of time in—I want her so badly, and I'm so horny, I don't know how much more I can take.

I position myself over her nude body so my throbbing cock is knocking at the door of her drenched pussy.

I rub my tip on her cunt, getting it slick with her juices, and she comes to life again.

She has been refusing to look at me since her thunderous orgasm, but she can't avoid me for long.

I keep rubbing my head against her entrance, riling her up, and when she starts moaning again (and I'm about to lose it), I push my cock inside her.

I meant to tease her a little more and ease myself in slowly, but I want her enveloping my stiff length right now, so I bury my dick deep, relishing the sound of her crying out as I shove my cock all the way in.

She is deliciously tight and wet all around me.

I ease myself in and out, surrendering to her pussy massage.

I close my eyes and savor the feel of every part of her—her warm body beneath me, her slick inner flesh gripping me.

I increase my rhythm.

She rests a hand on my ass as I thrust into her with growing intensity, and the way she says, "Oh, Jake!" is different and reaches some part of my ear that seems directly connected to my sensitive dick, taking me close to the orgasmic edge, fast.

I start fucking her hard in a relentless rhythm while she screams my name.

As I drive into her juicy pussy, I bend my head to suck on her delicate neck.

The neck-kissing seems to drive her crazy, and I feel a wave of feminine juices wash over my throbbing cock, pushing me one step closer to the edge.

I want to shove my dick in and out of her all night,

but for now, the sights, sounds, and smells of her overwhelm me, and my cock is ready to explode.

She wraps her legs around me and squeezes me to her as I thrust even harder as I get milked, shooting my cum up her pussy in spout after spout.

I feel her pulsating against me in a way that lets me know she came again, and we flood each other with juices, squeezing out every morsel of pleasure as we both throb, our bodies tightening in final contractions.

I collapse on top of her when it's over, trapping her beneath me, and I intend to keep her there as long as I can.

I feel her arms wrap around me, and another sort of warmth washes over me.

I awaken to odd movements, and before everything comes back to me, I stop Gina before she escapes the bed.

"Where the hell do you think you're going?" I ask, and when her eyes meet mine, I see a change come over her I can't identify.

"Water," she says, and I'm not sure I believe her, so I get up too.

"You don't have to..."

"I want to," I say, and I move her along when she attempts to grab her clothes. She better get used to being naked around me.

I can tell she's got a lot tossing around her head as we head to the kitchen, and I want to assure her that what we did wasn't just some casual thing—I didn't just want to scratch an itch, and she wasn't just the convenient means to do so.

"I think *you* should stay here," I say. "No more tenants."

She looks at me strangely but doesn't answer.

She pours a glass of water, and then wordlessly asks me if I want one.

I shake my head, and she closes the fridge.

"You're the ideal tenant," I continue as she gulps down the water. "Besides, it's much bigger than your place, and I'll get you whatever else you need..."

"But what would I do when you come back? I can't just keep hopping in and out of this place depending on your schedule."

"The whole point is that you don't leave, Gina. Stay here with me now, and stay with me if or when I get deployed again. Stay here and..." I want to say, "raise my baby," but I don't want to scare her—she might not be ready to accept that part yet. "All I do is think of you, Gina. I want you even closer to me, and even closer than this." I indicate our nudity and what we've just done.

There is something suddenly soft and vulnerable about her that's pulling at me, tugging at my heart. She is disturbing my spirit with her femininity in all its wonderful glory—she is driving me crazy! I can practically feel my testosterone levels rise as I respond to whatever crazy-making pheromones she's giving off.

I'm overwhelmed by the need to take care of her, protect her, and make sure she never has to worry about anything ever again. I want to make her happy, see her face soften with love and joy, give everything she is to me, and to share all ups and downs with her.

"What is it?" she asks, suddenly looking worried.

I realize I am visibly panting hard.

My cock has also blown up to size again, and among all the other things I want when it comes to her, I want to fuck her again right now.

I lift her onto the counter.

"Jake..."

"Say you'll stay with me, Gina—I need you," I say as I wrap her legs around me.

She shakes her head, and I position the tip of my engorged cock at her entrance.

"You're my best friend, Gina—always have been, always will be. I don't plan to stop doing this," I say as I push the head of my cock inside of her.

She leans her head back slightly, and when she looks back at me, her eyes have turned into dark pools.

I finally recognize what's been going on with her— the thing that has made her suddenly seem so soft and delicate.

"I love you too, Gina," I say, and it comes out like a whisper as my throat constricts a bit with emotion.

She flings her arms around my neck, and I feel her body relax in surrender to it all.

I push my dick all the way inside of her and start thrusting against the now-familiar warmth of her slick walls as they massage my length.

"I want everything with you, Gina, and I won't stop doing this until I get it. I won't stop then, either."

She lifts her gaze to my face, and when our eyes meet, I know she can see the truth in mine as I can see it in hers.

She brings her lips toward mine and I gratefully accept her soft kiss.

That extra intimate contact with her heightens the pleasure at my middle and I fuck her tight pussy more vigorously, slamming into her while holding her tightly to me, my hands cupping her delicious ass cheeks.

Her lips leave mine as she moans and leans her head back a little.

"God, I love you too, Jake," she says, and those words take me over the edge.

I dig into her in an increased rhythm, and she takes all my cum as I explode inside of her once again.

She holds on to me while I come down, and I think about all the days we have ahead of us—all the positions to try, and the places to try them in—and I swell with joy.

"So you will stay with me?" I say after a few seconds.

She kisses my cheek. "Of course, Jake. I'm always here for you. You know I'll do whatever you want."

Her words make me smile, and a golden warmth fills me.

And I might be crazy, but I feel as if my seed has already started to grow in her.

POSSESSED BY YOU

Brandon can't take it anymore. His sexy, longtime friend, Lola, needs to crash at his place for a while, and he's not sure how to handle his secret desire for her. He wants to *take advantage* of the situation, but he's not sure where to start. Lucky for him, his dilemma is taken care of by a sleep disorder, and Lola finds herself at the mercy of her old friend's lust!

1

BRANDON

Lola friend-zoned me a long time ago.

From the day I met her at eight years old on the playground in elementary school, and I tried to kiss her on the cheek, she drew the line in the sand. She clocked me so hard that, whenever I heard some dude hits like a girl, my first thought was that he could knock out a tooth.

Lola and I quickly got over our one-sided mini-scuffle, and we've been friends ever since—once I apologized to her and she made me promise not to try that shit again while she held me by the shirt.

Yes, eight-year-old Lola actually said those words: "Promise you won't try that shit again and I'll forgive you."

She still cusses like a sailor, and I eventually learned that she got it from her mom who, it became clear, never bothered with parenting her much.

Lola was allowed to do whatever: she snuck out at night and didn't get in trouble, she started drinking alcohol at fifteen; she experimented with various drugs. She even told me her mom was the one to introduce her to pot.

Anyway, things have remained platonic between us since that day on the playground, despite us getting so close over the years. She hasn't changed her mind about our friendship, but *my* mind never changed—I just mastered hiding my desire for her. I've endured not getting a chance to be with her because at least she lets me be around her as one of her closest friends; I'll take that for now.

I know I'm the first person she comes to see when she's in town, the first person she spills her guts to about how things are going in her life.

She's super adventurous and goes exploring one way or another—in this country or some other for various lengths of time—but she always comes back, and when she does, rushes to tell me all about her latest trip.

It's both torture and pleasure rolled into one to have her and not be able to have her.

She's been my friend forever, but I've wanted to plow her forever, too. I want to bury my dick balls-deep in her, but I can't tell her that; I can't let on in any way for fear she'd completely lock me out, and I'll lose the privileges I currently have.

The thought of no longer having the chance to

hear her voice as she tells me some crazy story is unbearable—my eyes live for the sight of her, my ears ache for her raspy but totally sexy voice as she calls to check in.

I may never get a chance to claim her in my bed, but in this small way, Lola is mine.

While her distance drives me crazy, Lola's proximity is even worse. At least when she's on the road, somewhere far away from me, I can distract myself. When she's near me and I can see her sweet, round face, and take in her soft, curvy body, or watch her chest rise and fall as she breathes, my brain gets a bit scrambled.

She is currently opposite me at my place, talking about her latest adventure, and all I can think about is how much I want to kiss those rapidly moving lips.

Her smile gives me joy like you wouldn't believe, and I dread the moment she decides we've chatted enough and heads for the door.

I wish I could keep her with me forever.

I greedily take in her form, noticing small changes.

Her hair is slightly longer now, for example, and her style of clothes has changed a bit.

She's still as beautiful as the day I met her, though back then, she had lighter skin, rounder cheeks, and awesomely thick, curly hair.

Now her skin's a glowing brown, and her cheeks are still round, but her hair is super straight.

She told me some time ago she relaxed it, then went on to explain what she meant and I checked out. I got the gist of it—she sort of permanently straightened her hair, and from what I know of her, she probably did it to blend in more with the folks around her.

She bugged her mom to let her do it for a while but kept being told it was an unnecessary expense, despite the teasing Lola got about her unruly curls. Her mom finally let her do it when she was fourteen, and she has kept it that way since.

Her mom made her pay for it from day one—Lola worked for neighbors or whoever would hire a fourteen-year-old.

Lola told me all of this like it makes a difference.

Whatever. I like her hair curly or straight, and I sure as hell don't care about an extra five or ten pounds. For god's sake, I've been in love with this girl since the day she punched me in the face.

But I knew what she looked like mattered to her a lot.

She grew up in a trailer park—the only child of a fair-skinned, blue-eyed blonde who couldn't guess who Lola's dad could be based on appearance since she'd fucked so many black guys.

Lola didn't end up white and everybody could see it, and she's had to endure all sorts of harsh looks and words because of it.

Still, Lola has always had a strong personality, a toughness about her that persisted despite all the things that fucked with her. She doesn't wallow in self-pity over anything; in fact, she'd tell me matter-of-factly about stuff that happened to her, and I'd sit there in horror or seething rage while she looks like she's telling me what the weather's like outside.

Although she's strong, she's been dealing with an identity crisis for a long time—beyond what most of us go through because of her status as the only brown girl among ignorant white trash.

To top it off, her mom eventually got arrested and sent to jail for a couple of charges, so Lola got sent to foster care at the age of sixteen, lived in a group home through eighteen, then got kicked out into the world for aging out of the system.

She's been wandering ever since.

Her mom's still in jail—at least for another year—and I know that despite all of Lola's excitement over potential adventures and not having any responsibilities, she feels lost and alone.

She needs some grounding, a purpose. She needs to know she's not alone, and I can help her out.

I can't believe my luck when Lola asks me for a favor at the end of our catch-up session.

Lola has been living sort of like a drifter, and she

has asked to stay with me for a week before she goes on her next road trip. Of course, I don't hesitate to grant her request.

"Thanks again for letting me crash here," says my beautiful couch-surfer extraordinaire.

Believe it or not, she has never crashed with me before, and I've tried not to think about it and take it personally when she found other people to crash with while in the area.

But now that she's actually here in front of me and will be within my reach for several days, I realize she's been doing me a favor all this time—consciously or unconsciously.

The fact that she'll be alone with me, on my couch and in a vulnerable position, is messing with my head. I can have my way with her, I realize, and finally find out what it's like to sink myself into her warmth, to plow her slick depths with my hungry cock.

I have to shake naughty thoughts off constantly now—thoughts involving slipping something into her drink so she doesn't wake up while I explore her body.

What's wrong with me? I'd want her to be aware of my every move, each plunge into her warm, feminine canal. I'd want to watch her lean her head back as she accepts the pleasure I can give.

But I learned something about myself during the aftermath of her request: I want Lola however I can get her.

I don't see how she stayed so clueless about my

desire for her, but it has worked in my favor since she still trusts me enough to sleep on my couch for several nights. She's going to let herself be alone with me, spend night upon night in my home.

Not that we haven't been alone before—she visited my home many times when we were teenagers, but it was always in the daytime. If we hung out together at night, it was always out somewhere—at a movie or (later) at a bar.

I have to be careful—I can't give myself away with my body language, and I certainly can't carry out the deep slumber fantasy because I don't want to drug her in case something reacts with her badly.

She'll be with me a whole week, so I have a little time to plot and plan how I'm going to take her, and I can't make any rash moves in the meantime.

But I have no doubt I will find a way.

Lola won't leave here without us knowing each other a whole lot better.

LOLA

Brandon's been acting a little weird.

He seems nervous for some reason—a little more nervous than usual.

He probably thinks he covered up his crush on me pretty well over the years, but he's so transparent; I have no doubt he still has feelings for me beyond friendship. No matter how nonchalant he acts, I'm aware he has a hard time being around me, that he still hasn't gotten over that crush from long ago.

I suppose I've made it worse, still being around him like this, dangling myself in front of him. But I figured with us graduating from high school he'd grow out of it, especially since he got to go to college and live out a whole life there without me in it. Once he graduated and we touched base again, however, it was like nothing changed.

I'm glad he still feels close to me; he's still my friend and always there for me.

There's something comforting about that—no matter where I go or how long I take to get back, he'll be waiting for me.

Once in a while, I get hit by fear that the next time I see him, he'll finally be over me and meet me with cold indifference.

Thankfully, that time has not yet arrived.

His hazel eyes are on me now, like he's watching my every move. It's as if he wants to drink me in—like he's afraid he'll miss something if he blinks.

His heart is plainly on his sleeve, and I'm so sorry to do this to him—to be physically even closer to him than before.

He looks like he can barely handle my nearness now, much less my continued presence for a week straight in his home, crashing on his couch.

I've tried to spare him this—spare us both—but I'm finally at a point where I have nowhere else to turn. I can't tell him that, of course—I can't let him know he was my last resort when all my other options fell through.

I'm sort of relieved he ended up being my shelter though.

He offered me his bed, but I had to turn it down. Best to keep things as friendly as possible, and that means not having anything at all to do with his bed.

I'm so used to couches anyway, and his is particularly comfy.

The quality of his couch isn't the only thing I've noticed—his whole quality of life seems to have changed.

Before, he lived in his parents' place in a neighborhood of people who pretended to be solidly middle-class, but were more lower-middle-class.

Now he's in a neighborhood of undoubtedly middle-class people, with probably some upper-middle-class folks sprinkled in.

There's a noticeable difference in the landscaping, the clothes, the cars.

The place his parents left him when they died in a car accident a few years ago was smaller than his place now, and it had more rooms squashed into it.

Now, he's got this huge bachelor pad with every creature comfort you can imagine.

I also realized there's something more confident about him—like he picked up a bit of swagger, and I'm finding it pretty sexy. He was always fairly good-looking, though not my type, but he's suddenly now a lot more attractive.

I wonder what's the deal?

Maybe he has a new job or something that pays him pretty well and he's able to 'move on up,' so he's feeling himself, living life like a big ol' pimp.

I realize I've been yapping about myself and haven't gotten anything out of him about his life lately.

I noticed the lack of a girlfriend around, but what else?

"So," I begin, "what have you been up to, Mr. I-Live-In-A-Much-Bigger-Place-Now?" I ask.

He smiles briefly before he answers.

"I made some good investments," he says. "I pretty much don't have to work anymore, so if you hang around here in the day, I'm afraid you'll bump into me a lot—though I go out here and there on some errand or other. Anyway, I should warn you: my sleepwalking has gotten a bit worse. Don't be alarmed if you see me walking into the kitchen late at night and I don't respond to you talking to me or anything. Definitely don't let me just walk out the door if I head for it—I can still function and perform the task of unlocking it, so just guide me gently back to my room. Whatever you do, don't try to wake me. But don't worry too much about it either, I probably won't bother you." He stands and I realize he's preparing to leave.

It registers that it's now dark outside. Time sure flew!

"Be back with your blankets, etc.," he says, then turns to go. I find myself watching him till he's out of sight, and I try to ignore how much I like what I see.

He returns with an armful of bed linens and pillows, then dumps them on the couch.

"Anyway, good night," he says. "Maybe we can do breakfast or something in the morning. We can even go to your favorite place—Denny's—if you want."

"That sounds nice," I say, then quickly turn from him to prepare to watch TV until I fall asleep.

~

I awaken to a sound and realize Brandon's in the kitchen, grabbing some water.

I settle back into my spot and try to go back to sleep, not bothering to figure out if he's actually awake or not. But what makes it harder is knowing he's there, just a few feet away, so I have to wait until he heads back to his room to relax into sleep again.

Brandon doesn't head back to his room, however.

I turn back toward him and realize he's sort of staring in my direction, and a prickling sensation runs through my body.

I figure he must be sleepwalking since I'm now looking at him directly and he's not looking away, embarrassed at having been caught. He's almost looking right through me.

I take a moment to take in his shirtless torso and realize he must have been hitting the gym pretty hard —his body is ridiculously hot with those muscled arms and those washboard abs.

He looked a bit more fit to me when we chatted yesterday, but seeing his exposed muscles now, so hard and defined, is turning me on a little, especially with his hazel eyes stuck on me.

My pussy starts tingling.

Then Brandon heads for me, and it tingles more.

"Hey, Brandon," I whisper, trying to reach some part of him, but he doesn't respond.

"Brandon!" I whisper harder, but I know I'm in trouble as he reaches the couch and his expression hasn't changed.

Okay, he said to guide him back to his room gently, I remember, but it goes out the window when he suddenly climbs on top of me, pushing me back into the couch.

His hands reach the sides of my hips, and he quickly pulls my panties down and flings them aside.

My heart is jackhammering against my chest in panic.

How do I stop this guy?

The answer is that I don't—I can't! He is too strong, and lucky for me, instead of whipping his cock out of his boxers and shoving it between my legs like I know Awake Brandon wants to do so badly, Sleep Brandon buries his face in my pussy.

All the fight in me evaporates and my mind blanks at the delicious sensation of his lips on my most sensitive parts, his tongue flicking over my folds.

All I can do is lie back and enjoy my best friend lapping at my sensitive pussy, my body arching and twisting as he masterfully licks me into a frenzy, torturing me with his skillful mouth.

I can't help myself as I moan in pleasure from his teases, his tongue grazing my clit here and licking my entrance there. His lips pull at my flesh hungrily, and his tongue wags at my desperate, aching parts until they can't take it anymore. His mouth takes me to explosive completion, my hips thrusting to take the last bit of pleasure from his mouth.

I can't think properly when it's all over as my brain shuts down, but eventually, I remember what usually comes next. I wonder if he's going to take me right here, right now, while completely under the grip of sleep?

I realize I don't mind the idea at all—it means I can have my cake and eat it too. My suddenly hot buddy can fuck my brains out and satisfy this burning need I have, and in the morning, we get to still be just friends; he won't realize what we've done.

I can keep a secret, and I know I'll have to. I don't think he can handle things changing between us, and while I'd be happy to keep things casual despite knowing him intimately, if Brandon finds out about what we've done, everything *will* change, and I don't want it to.

As I eagerly adjust myself to encourage him to continue, he finally pulls his head away from my throbbing center, extracting his body from the couch, then calmly walks back toward his bedroom.

I stare after him in shock.

3

―――

BRANDON

Man, I had a vivid dream about Lola last night —I even awoke with a faint taste of pussy on my lips.

Morning wood is here to greet me this morning after those filthy fantasies; I need to figure out a plan fast to get Lola in my bed and satisfy my needy dick.

I can flash my new money around, but would that work with her?

I told her I made a good investment, but what I meant was, I invested five dollars in lotto tickets and ended up with a winning one.

Now that I have millions at my disposal, I can take care of Lola's every need, but how do I convince her of that?

My thoughts are interrupted by the sound of the shower turning on.

I relax back into the bed, grab my cock, and

prepare to service myself while thinking of beautiful Lola in the shower, water dripping down her soft, curvy body, making pathways down her ample boobs, her abdomen, dripping from her sweet pussy lips.

I tug myself more furiously.

My fantasy gets more elaborate, and I'm suddenly in the shower with her, taking in her wet body with my eyes, then taking one of her breasts in my mouth. One of my hands finds its way to a juicy ass cheek and I squeeze it, then lower myself until I'm facing her womanly core. I start to lick her, making her moan deliciously, delighting in hearing her whisper my name as her hands grab my hair, and her center gets wetter as she pulls me closer.

Then I imagine her stopping my tongue teases to offer me the same, bending to enclose her juicy mouth over my hard, raging cock.

When I guide her to stand back up, I turn her around and make her plant her hands on the shower wall as she bends her juicy ass toward me.

Then I point my dick at her slick entrance, burying myself in her pussy from behind.

I plow her mercilessly until I'm pumping warm, creamy fluid into her.

My hands furiously work my throbbing cock, and I'm spilling my seed on my bed in moments.

The shower turns off and I stay in place until I'm sure Lola is dressed.

I strip my sheets, preparing to change them for

tonight so Lola has a clean set to lie on if we make it back here.

Chances are, though, I'll end up fucking her on that couch.

"Hope I didn't do anything weird in my sleep," I say as we face each other, picking up the Denny's menu.

Lola looks at me strangely, and I don't know what to make of it.

"Wait, did I?" I ask, suddenly concerned.

"Oh, you came out and got some water," she says casually, but her manner says otherwise. She seems nervous, and I realize she sort of stuttered her words, but I'm not sure what that means.

Did I scare her somehow?

I ask her aloud, and she shakes her head.

"You were the perfect gentleman," she says with a sly sort of smile.

"See? I told you you had nothing to worry about," I say, but an idea suddenly occurs to me.

I've already told her to expect strange actions; I've already primed her for uncharacteristic behavior from me. Basically, I already planted one seed, and later tonight, using all the acting skills I can muster, I'll plant another.

Lola is finally going to get what's been coming to

her for a long time now that I've finally figured out how to pull it off.

~

I have to wait a while.

Lola disappears for the day, then when she returns in the evening, I treat her to a *very* nice dinner.

"Must've been a damned good investment," she says, and I bite my tongue so I don't mention my new financial status.

To be honest, I don't care if she uses me for my money if it means I get to be with her for a while; I'd get a real chance to win her heart.

I only want to see a small indication, a spark of interest from her first so I don't expect the worst the whole time I'm with her.

Then again, considering my plans tonight, I aim to keep Lola in my life in a way that won't allow her to get away from me as easily.

When we get back to my place, we hang out watching TV, then I prepare to retire to my bedroom.

I'm not sure if it's in my head or not, but Lola gives me a sort of wistful look as I leave—like she's not ready for me to go yet.

But that's part of my plan, too—always leave her wanting more.

I read a book for a while, waiting for the sound of the TV turning off, then I wait a bit longer.

Finally, after hours of waiting for the right moment, I make my way to the kitchen.

Step one: go for water while appearing to be in a daze.

Step two: go for Lola.

I feel Lola's eyes on me as I go through the motions.

She seems slightly nervous but quite aware and very interested.

I finish drinking the water, put my glass down. then look in her direction.

She is breathing hard—like she's expecting something to go down.

I walk toward her, a ball of nerves myself, but then Lola does the most wondrous thing, almost knocking me completely out of character: she relaxes back into the couch, opening her legs so that I can see her pussy. She decided to sleep with just a T-shirt on.

My cock springs to attention.

I get the feeling she wants me to lick her there so I indulge her, bending to her sweet core, unable to believe what's happening.

Is this a dream after all?

Either way, I have no intention of stopping.

I lap at her until I can't take it anymore, then I get in position to stuff my cock in her.

But then she grabs my shoulders in a sort of stopping gesture.

Too bad she thinks she can actually stop me!

I continue to play up my dazed state while I yank her T-shirt off.

She had still been fairly calm until I did that.

"Brandon!" she whispers in a sort of panicked voice.

I bring my lips to her neck and feel her lean her head back as she moans.

She still struggles against me a bit, but she has no chance of escaping my grip on her wrists, and no chance of throwing me.

She is trapped beneath me.

"Brandon, wait—wake up!" she says. "I've changed my mind!"

I have no idea what she's talking about and I don't care.

Instead, I hover over her in response, preparing to take her at last.

I'm already naked since I didn't want to make too much work for myself, and I part her legs so I can rest between them.

"Oh my god," she says, "this will change everything for me!"

She tries to get loose again.

Good luck with that!

My cock is hard and throbbing, demanding I get inside of her at once.

But now that her lovely breasts are exposed to me, I want a taste, so I bend to suck each of them.

"Oh god," she whimpers, accepting each lick and suck, her moans and gasps driving me crazy.

Her skin is so soft, and the scent of her makes my cock throb even more.

Too many of my senses are being stimulated, and I truly can't take it anymore.

"Brandon!" she whispers one last time, and I distract her by bringing my lips down on hers. As I explore her warm, wet mouth with mine, my dick finds her other warm, wet mouth and I push myself into her.

She arches her back in response and we both let out a groan, mine filled with pleasure.

I slide in some more, making her take every inch of me, then I start moving in and out of her slick, welcoming canal, her inner walls clutching at me and making me want to fuck her even harder.

There's no going back now.

4

—

LOLA

Things happened so fast.

Brandon fucks me mercilessly, plowing my insides with his thick cock, grinding against me in delicious ways.

I grab him to me, running my hands down his sinewy body every now and then, enjoying the feel of his contracting muscles as he digs into my pussy.

I allow myself to take all of him in and relax into the pleasure, the joy he's giving me.

When his pace quickens, my body follows his ascent to climax.

He fucks me harder and faster, and my body thrusts, rising to meet him.

I realize he's about to come inside me, so I try to get him to pull out but fail. I resign to having his juices fill me as my orgasmic river floods him.

We lie there, panting. Sated. Delirious with pleasure.

Brandon feels amazing inside me, and now I'm longing for much more with him.

I don't want things to stop here, and I don't want to be the only one who knows about this.

I feel vulnerable to him now.

Somewhere along the way of reacquainting myself with my old friend, I realized how much I rely on him to always be there for me, how much of a comfort our close friendship is. How much of a mess I'd be if anything happened to end it.

It was a dangerous place to end up because now, after having him fuck me, I feel even more connected to him.

I was fine the night before and could have maintained the necessary distance, but something changed today in our moments together and opened me up to him.

His love for me pierced my armor, and our easy comfort with each other sank in even deeper. I realized that Brandon is the best thing about my life.

Now, he is stirring, and I know he's about to leave me to go back to his room.

My heart sinks. I don't want him to go—not now, not ever.

"Stay," I whisper, knowing Sleep Brandon will do what he wants and return to his room as before, leaving me to my torturous thoughts and a restless, lonely night.

But to my surprise, Brandon stays in place; he even adjusts our bodies and his arms so that I'm wrapped in them.

My heart soars.

Nothing that I've experienced in the entire world feels better than this.

We both stir when morning comes, and I immediately flush with embarrassment as our nakedness registers.

What am I supposed to say? "Hey, bud, you sleep-fucked me!" Yeah, right.

Brandon opens his eyes and looks around. Then he looks back at me with worry. He starts to get up, and I let him, still not knowing what to say.

"What happened here?" he asks, wrapping one of the many sheets around him. I quickly cover myself with another.

How do I put this? Who do I blame?

"We both had very vivid dreams that turned out not to be dreams," I say lamely.

His face reflects confusion, then a slow understanding.

"Wait a minute—did this happen before? Two nights ago? Did I do more than get water in my sleep that night?"

I nod. "But not like all the way. Not like... last night."

He looks distressed. "Why didn't you tell me?" he asks, his lovely eyes wide.

I shrug, feeling worried; I don't want him to get mad at me. "Well, I figured you didn't know, so there was no need to mention it. No harm, no foul. Anyway, I pretty much had no choice but to let you do your thing."

"God, I'm so sorry, Lola," he says.

"Don't be," I reply, yanking his sheet from him.

I grab his hand and pull him back down on the couch, then straddle myself above him.

Before he covered himself with the sheet, I noticed he had a stiffy, and my body wants it buried in me more than anything else right now.

"Wait, Lola—are you sure...?"

"More than anything, Brandon. I want you inside me. Again. I couldn't stop you the other night or last night, partly because I didn't want to."

I position my wet, tingling pussy over his hard dick, then lower myself on it.

"Oh, Lola," he says with a masculine groan, the sound turning me on even more.

His large, strong hands find my butt cheeks and grips them.

Once he's all the way inside, I start moving on top of him, my breasts bouncing against his chest.

He leans his head back, looking the picture of ecstasy.

"You have no idea how long I've wanted this, Lola," he says.

"I think I do," I say as I continue to ride him.

I rub my clit against his pelvis while moving up and down his shaft, bringing myself closer to clitoral orgasm while his hands support my ass, pushing me harder against him every now and then.

His dick fills me deliciously, and I near the edge of climax.

Brandon is rolling all sorts of dirty, nasty words off his tongue, praising my breasts and pussy.

In no time, our enjoyment of each other takes me to climax, and I squeeze my body against his.

He bounces me harder on him until his dick is pulsating inside me, emptying cum into my canal.

We stay entwined, pulsing against each other and breathing hard as we both come down.

"What the hell changed your mind?" he asks eventually, his voice gentle. "Though obviously, I'm not complaining."

I let out a breath before answering. "There's something different about you, and I find it irresistible. Plus, I've come to appreciate our friendship, our closeness even more. And then you gave me the best oral sex of my life while completely asleep! Guess I had no chance, really."

He grins. Then his face sobers up.

"I have a confession to make," he says.

My heart stills. "Shoot," I say, fearful of his next words.

"I was completely out of it the first night, so I don't remember anything—although I did awake with the taste of pussy in my mouth. But I thought I'd dreamt of eating you, so I just chalked it up to that. Last night, however, I was awake the entire time."

His hazel eyes lock on my face in utter seriousness, like he's expecting me to get mad and storm off, breaking things off between us forever.

I lightly slap him on the shoulder.

"You dirty boy," I say with a smile. "You broke your... what is it now... sixteen-year-old promise!"

He laughs heartily. "Yes, eight-year-old me *did* promise eight-year-old you that I wouldn't come on to you again—but that only stood for as long as you didn't want it. I'm afraid the moment you let me lick you to orgasm, all bets were off."

I smile at him.

He is now softening inside me, and I know we'll have to disentangle soon.

"So what does all of this mean?" I ask, looking at him with unspoken words in my eyes.

"It means," he begins, wrapping his arms around my waist, "that you're mine now."

"Excuse me?"

"It means you'll take my cock whenever I want to give it to you, and that hopefully, you don't need to wander anymore. Your home is here with me, Lola, and there's nothing I'd like more than to make another you—wild, curly hair and all, clocking fast dudes on playgrounds. Except this time, both Daddy and Mommy will be there unconditionally, backing her up every step of the way so she never feels lost."

I'm on the verge of tears, and they quickly fill my eyes and fall down my cheeks before I realize it.

I'm not on the pill, so there's a very real chance Brandon put a baby in me, and the thought doesn't scare me like I once thought it would.

"I can take care of you, Lola—I have more money than we'll ever need, and you don't have to sleep on another couch again." His hand cups my cheek and a finger caresses it. I'm not sure if he was just caressing me or wiping away a tear. Probably both.

He smiles at me, his eyes saying all. "I love you, Lola—always have, always will. You're home now. You're staying with me."

I finally burst into tears and laughter, and I grab him into a tight hug.

Brandon holds me in a way that emphasizes his words—a protective, loving embrace that tells me all I need to know.

I am safe with him.

When we finally disentangle ourselves, I'm still

filled with emotion, and it has fused itself with other parts of me, heightening other sensations.

Despite what we did just ten minutes ago, I have no doubt, as we head to the shower, we'll be doing it all over again soon.

CLAIMED BY YOU

Curvy, untouched Janine thinks she's ready for the next important step in her womanhood, so she's on the lookout for a strong alpha male to give her innocence to. Her best friend, Josh, lives a few houses away, and when she pops by to visit him, she runs into a hot, muscular guy leaving his place and thinks he's the one. She asks Josh to hook her up with the hunky stranger and Josh agrees, but he suddenly realizes *he* should be the one to get the voluptuous brown beauty's gift, and he'll make sure to stuff his sexy best friend *first*!

1

———

JANINE

I know I'm not exactly everyone's type, but any guy who finds my size intimidating, I just figure he has a small dick. So go on, Mr. Tiny Penis—remove yourself from my pool of possibilities because my hips appear too wide, and you can't imagine your tiny wiener dwarfed even more by my ample curves. No skin off my back.

Either way, I'm still a virgin, and I wouldn't know what to compare the guy's dick to.

I don't watch porn or anything, and I haven't seen a guy's penis since fourth grade when some dude in my class whipped his dick out to show me after the teacher stepped out for a moment.

"Now show me yours," he said afterward, grinning like a fool, and I turned away from him in disgust.

I definitely wasn't interested in boy parts back then, but at the age of twenty, I'm interested now!

It seems I'm the last of my friends to have no experience still, and my longing to find out what it's like to have a cock inside me has skyrocketed.

It's sort of a frightening idea—sharing your body with someone that way—an unprecedented vulnerability. But I'm ready.

Rubbing my clit when it tingles is one thing, but there's one place I can't quite reach: deep inside me, made for a dick's penetration.

I'm not into sex toys either; I want the real thing with a *real* man—a strong, confident alpha male who can handle all of me.

The man who gets me won't be intimidated by what I have to offer, and skinny or stocky, he'll love watching his thick cock get lost in me.

I'm not sure how this whole thing's going to work out exactly because I have absolutely no one in mind, but I'll find someone soon. I hope.

I definitely don't want to be like a cousin of mine who's still a virgin at the age of twenty-nine!

In a brief moment of desperation, I even considered doing it with my best friend, Josh, but a guy of average height and weight with average haircuts and ambitions doesn't exactly move me. Josh is fit and all, but with his dirty blond hair and blue eyes, he just isn't my type. I like guys with darker features: darker hair, darker skin.

Plus, Josh just doesn't have that kind of energy about him—the overwhelmingly masculine vibe that never lets you forget you're a puny girl.

I like men who can make me feel feminine and delicate, and Josh has never given me caveman, throw-you-over-the-shoulder vibes, so I've never been interested in him that way—thankfully, I guess, since I really appreciate his friendship.

Some people might think I'm being outrageously or unrealistically picky being an average girl myself, but where I live, I'm not actually average. Not many people around have my skin color, and these huge boobs of mine sure as hell can't be taken for granted—nothing about them is average.

Plus, my waist to hip ratio is crazy. I'm one of those 'big-boned' weirdos with a large frame, but a small waist, beautifully in proportion to my large tits and round ass. I've got the kind of body men used to make statues of—a Rubenesque goddess like Anna Nicole Smith or Tocarra Jones.

Well, that's what I tell myself—that the lack of men approaching me is due to intimidation. They look away or avoid eye contact with me 'cause they can't handle it—their brain might short circuit from all this juicy femininity. And some of them, well, they're walking with their girlfriends, so they make sure not to accidentally disrespect her by ogling me.

Some guys could even get in trouble with their parents for dating a girl like me; it's best to play it safe and take home a fair-skinned blonde or redhead.

So there you have it—being surrounded by

cowards is how I ended up here: single, virginal, and unsure of my prospects.

I sort of know what I want in a guy, but I haven't seen a lot of it represented here.

And I've been pretty sheltered up to this point—I've never gone beyond thirty miles from home.

I had the perfect opportunity to finally venture out and live somewhere new for college, but I stuck with a local one.

So I guess, in a way, I've been a bit of a coward myself.

Well, it's time to spread my wings... and other things.

In the meantime, since today's a Saturday and I don't have classes or anything, I'm going to hang out with my friend, Josh.

He lives a few houses away and we've been friends since my mom and I moved here about ten years ago, so he's an easy distraction from all my naughty thoughts.

Maybe he can even help me come up with someone to hook up with!

He's pretty much the only guy friend I have, and there's probably some single hot dude he knows from his job or something he could introduce me to.

Looks like I'm in luck!

When I get to Josh's place, the door opens before I can knock, and a chocolate hunk walks out, flashing me a brief but beautiful smile.

I watch him and his tight ass until I can see no more of his handsome face with that white-teethed grin and all those muscles disappear as his car drives off.

I have to fan myself once I step inside Josh's place and his door closes behind me.

I finally focus on my blue-eyed friend.

"Phew!" I say. "Okay, details please. Who the hell was that?"

"Who, Jermaine?"

"Yes, fine-ass Jermaine. You've been holding out on me, Josh. I didn't know you had friends like that!"

"Well, he's not exactly my friend—he's a client."

Of course. I should have guessed that. Josh works at a gym and offers personal training even in his off hours.

Either way, this Jermaine's exactly my type. He's like a darker version of Dwayne "The Rock" Johnson, but The Rock is pretty much everybody's type, right? All hard and strong and masculine and... phew! My face is hot.

"He's an aspiring actor," Josh continues, "and he's got an agent who told him to bulk up a little before he submits him for this soap opera role. Anyway, I got this new video game..."

"Oh, hell no—you're not changing the subject. You need to set me up with Jermaine."

"Come on, Janine."

"Don't play—set me up with him! He's fine as hell, and if I'm gonna finally give it up to someone, I want that someone to be fine as hell. No regrets. Even if his dick isn't all that big, because what the hell would I know? I'm still a virgin. So hook a sister up, Josh, please and thank you!"

"Whoa, whoa, whoa. Think about this carefully. You don't even know much about him."

"I don't have to—I already told you my purpose for him. Besides, you've told me enough. He might be some broke-ass artist... although not if he's hiring you, right? Either way, I just need to scratch an itch and he looks like the perfect man for the job."

Josh is still hesitating, looking strange.

The hell is his problem?

"Wait, is he gay or something?" I wonder aloud.

"No, I just... this is a surprise is all. You've never asked me to set you up before. Well, there was that one time like four years ago, but you punked out! And you've always been so shy... I guess I'm just shocked."

"Okay, now get over it and let's get the ball rolling. Unless he has a girlfriend or something?" I give him a questioning look.

Josh shakes his head, still looking kind of bothered. "Far as I know he's available."

I now give him a very pointed look, and he lets out

a heavy breath like I'm asking him to lend me some damn money.

"Fine, I'll do my best," he says, not looking happy about it at all.

I smile at him. "Great. Now, what's this new game you got?"

2

JOSH

I don't know what got into me, but the minute Janine expressed interest in Jermaine, a ball of rage built in my body.

It's not like I even see her that way to get jealous!

Maybe it was the part where she said she's a virgin.

To be honest, I didn't know—we don't talk about stuff like that, though we talk about everything else.

In any case, there's practically nothing more mouthwatering than being faced with an untouched girl. All the possibilities swim before you: being the first to explore the territory, having the chance to leave a mark, the anticipation of a cock squeeze you can't believe from those extra tight walls.

A tiny percentage of men would flee from the prospect, afraid of the crazy that could come with it due to experiences with clingy chicks after they give it up, but those dumb-asses should always expect crazy and clingy so I say, just go for it.

A virgin is that rare prize, an opportunity to be the one and only. It feeds our egos to the brim! And, of course, the pleasure of diving into an untouched canal that grips your cock with a firmness makes you want to come in no time.

Some chicks think they need to do more than just lie there, which you expect of more experienced girls, but a virgin never has to worry—her body does all the work for her. Once you start sliding your dick in and out of that super tight warmth...

Fuck, I'm getting horny thinking about it; my cock is swelling.

Suddenly, I want to slip my dick between Janine's juicy legs, feel her arms wrapped around me as I plunge into her virgin pussy. I want to feel all of her soft, warm, feminine parts against my hard body, grab her big-ass boobs while pushing my engorged cock in and out of her tightness. I want to hear the slapping of our skin as I plow her until I'm blasting cum inside of her.

She's probably totally unaware of my filthy thoughts as she watches me walk through my latest video game, but I'm preoccupied the whole time I play, keenly aware of her delicate body next to mine and how much I want to claim it.

What the hell's wrong with me? Just because she said she wants to be with someone else?

She has casually mentioned being interested in people I knew before, but they were harmless little crushes she was too shy or whatever to do anything about.

This time, it's definitely different; she's serious. And not only is she serious about getting with some guy, she wants to *get with* him!

I don't know why the thought of Janine wanting Jermaine that way makes me so mad. It even annoys me that their names sort of sound alike.

Not to mention the thought of Jermaine's grubby hands actually on her—it makes me want to punch him in the face the next time I see him, and he hasn't even done anything.

Of course, his hands aren't literally grubby, and Janine's not exactly mine, but in a way she is, and I guess I'm just now seeing how possessive I am of her.

She's my friend, my beautiful curvy neighbor. I've been here all this time in her life, as she has been in mine—a whole decade.

I should be the one to caress her soft brown skin and grab all her cushiony, delicate parts. She should be offering that sweet virginal pussy up to *me*.

I know I'm being completely irrational. Janine and I are just friends—always have been. Before today, I never even saw her as anything but a convenient, nearby buddy with an appreciation for role-playing video games. Although honestly, in the back of our heads, guys are always open to a bit more than friendship from a girl around them, no matter what she looks like. Unless she's really a troll, which most girls aren't. I'll even venture to say most guys deliberately become friends with girls they don't mind one day sleeping with.

Anyway, what am I supposed to do now? Refuse to set her up?

I don't want to look like an asshole or give her any idea how all of this is affecting me.

I need to find a way to make Jermaine look bad—I can't let Janine know how much the thought of her with another guy bothers me.

When she's tired of watching me play and gets ready to try the game herself, I've figured out something that might change her mind.

"Listen, Janine, Jermaine's a player. He'd totally hit it and quit it."

"Duh! Isn't that what I pretty much explained? I want a dude I have no connection to. Tap it and tap out is ideal for me, I think, seeing how attached some chicks get to their firsts. And relationships with firsts pretty much never work out from what I've observed. Maybe two percent or something. Anyway, I just want a fine dude to do me so I can move on and look for a real relationship with clearer eyes."

"I don't really understand that. Don't you think it's best to do it with someone you actually like?"

"Oh, I like Jermaine," she says, wriggling her eyebrows at me ridiculously.

"No, I mean beyond liking what you see. Do you think chicks regret getting their cherry popped by someone they had feelings for, even if it doesn't work out in the end?"

"Well, damn, why do you care so much?" she says, suddenly frowning at me.

I soften my voice. "Look, I feel a bit protective toward you—you're like a sister to me. I just don't want to see you get hurt."

She relaxes again and smiles a little. "Well, I appreciate that, but *my* twat, *my* rules. Now set me up with Jermaine, pronto."

I'm having a particularly hard day today, and yes, I mean that in every sense of the word.

I had a dream about Janine last night—a dream that made everything worse, presenting her to me as this unbelievably sexy, horny, irresistible girl with eyes only for me. I actually got to screw her, and it took place in heaven or something—I don't know, lots of golden light and heavenly hosts background sounds. Probably influenced by that BioShock game I played yesterday after Janine left.

But before she left, Janine made me text Jermaine to let him know of her interest in him. Now they're out together, less than one day later—like they couldn't make a date fast enough.

What the hell did I agree to this shit for?

I stupidly tried to prove to myself I wasn't a selfish dick and a bad friend by going ahead with setting her up, and now I'm practically pulling out my hair. I have so many violent emotions raging through me, I don't recognize myself.

I'm jealous—jealous as fuck.

I don't know how I'm supposed to work with Jermaine after this—I want to punch him *through* the face for touching Janine, and since we're on the subject? How much touching will he get to do today exactly?

How Janine could pick him over me is beyond me —I've been here the whole time; I could have taken care of that virginity problem for her.

I know I'm not supposed to be thinking this way, but fuck it. Janine is mine, damn it—*mine*.

Excruciating hours pass while I wait to hear from her by phone or having her drop by to tell me all about her fucking date.

When my cell finally buzzes with a text from her, conflicting emotions jolt me at once: joy and anger.

I'm glad I'll be seeing her soon, but I also feel like she's a traitor now. She betrayed me by offering her body to someone else.

When I open the door to a smiling Janine, I immediately know she's in trouble. My emotions haven't calmed down a single bit, although they've taken a more positive turn.

I still feel possessive as hell, and I'm mad at her betrayal, but I still want her in very specific ways.

As she steps into my place, I get hit with the certainty I'm going to have her, no matter what happened in the hours before.

I force my voice to sound light, but my words come out through gritted teeth.

"So how did it go?"

She smiles and I get even madder.

"It was actually really nice. He's attractive and everything, and we got along well, but... I just couldn't do it."

My heart is thumping against my chest. "What do you mean?"

"Don't get me wrong—he's super hot, and if there's no emotional connection, the person should at least be hot and get you all bothered, right? And yes, I was horny, but I guess I just got scared. I don't know why. He's pretty much exactly what I was hoping for."

Again, opposite emotions pull at me—happiness and outrage. Happiness because... well, fuck yeah, he didn't get to be with her! And outrage that she said he was exactly what she was hoping for. What the hell am I, chopped liver?

"What do you think was missing, ultimately?"

I'm amazed at my ability to pretend like all is well when there's a tornado churning in me.

She shrugs. "I guess I'm not ready after all. Just that simple."

I'm still struggling—particularly with the part of me that was so sure I'd take her as soon as the next chance arrived, and here it is.

My cock is painfully at attention, and I'm surprised she hasn't picked up on it yet, but I guess she's so busy yapping about the details of her lame-ass date.

I mean, Jermaine only got a kiss on the cheek from her? Ha!

I need to get inside of her and erase all thoughts of him—she's better off with me than anybody.

I'm almost at the point where I can't turn back from these thoughts—I've lost most of my control, and watching her ample boobs move as she gestures isn't doing anything to help the situation. All I can do is imagine putting my hands on her shoulders, sliding them down her arms, then grabbing those delicious boobs. And burying my cock in her tight pussy, but later; first, I want to bring her body close to mine and feel her generous breasts squashed against me.

I can practically taste her now!

But a small part of me—I guess the part that's really her friend—doesn't want to ruin everything.

"I'm gonna need you to leave," I suddenly say to her.

3

JANINE

I stop talking immediately.

Lord knows I've been yapping for probably five minutes straight, but I'd been jumping around talking about neutral and even silly things. Josh couldn't have just gotten bored, then decided to rudely kick me out, could he?

Maybe it was something I said earlier.

I ran over everything talked about in the past few minutes, then realized I couldn't have possibly offended him.

"Why are you kicking me out? Did I say something wrong?"

"Janine, I will say this one more time: it's best if you leave my house right now; check with me tomorrow."

Now how can I possibly up and leave with no clue why I'm suddenly being evicted?

I keep pondering the possibilities, but then a

movement catches my eye, and I realize Josh's hand is over his crotch area.

The look in his eyes finally makes sense—he has a generous handful of erection.

Suddenly, I'm seeing him in a new light—with his blue eyes intense and not moving from me, I feel like prey, and I realize I like it!

He takes a step forward, and I step back.

My self-preservation instincts kick in, and I get ready to haul ass out of there.

Josh didn't need to say what would happen if I didn't leave right away—that much was clear—and I'm not ready for this.

Still, he's a grown man—couldn't he have contained himself a little longer or find a more gentlemanly way to get me to leave? Did he really need to hold his organ like a weapon with a promise in his eyes?

"Fuck, Janine—it's too late now."

His quick steps reach me, and I'm suddenly in his arms, pressed against him.

"Okay, you might be used to getting whatever you want, but you can't have me," I say, surprised at his iron grip.

"Well, that's up to me, isn't it?"

My heart practically stops. "What do you mean?" I ask in an embarrassingly shaky voice.

"Well, you're in my apartment, aren't you? And I'm stronger than you. You can run or try to fight all you want, but if I want you, I'll have you. Therefore, I meant exactly what I said—it's up to me, and guess what? I want you."

He starts working at my top, trying to get it off.

"Josh, what are you doing?" I demand. He flings my top aside. "Seriously, what are you doing?"

"I'm granting your wish, Janine. You want this, don't you? You come here, still untouched after telling me how much you want to get broken in—how else am I supposed to take it? There's no way I'm letting you give it up to Jermaine now."

"Josh, come on—you're my friend. I was just venting about that stuff—not asking you to hump me!"

Josh sort of giggles. "Hump? I'm going to fuck you, Janine, so you better get used to the idea."

My pussy tingles furiously.

"No, we can't do that to us! I know how these things go. Things'll change..."

"You don't know anything about this stuff—you're a virgin, and I'm here to teach you. You'll take everything I have to give you, and I mean that."

As if to punctuate his words, he works at my jeans, leading me to panic. Not that I thought he was playing before, but things are getting serious. In no time, I'll be before him in just my bra and panties—or just my bra if he manages to pull my panties down with my jeans, fully exposing me.

I must admit, though—this forceful side of him is turning me all the way on.

But there's no way I can let him go through with this; we're meant to be just friends.

"Please, Josh. Think about what you're doing…"

"I have, for a while now. The moment you told me you wanted Jermaine, I knew I had to have you."

"Oh, so you just don't want anyone else to be with me."

"No—I didn't realize how much I wanted you until it became clear someone else might take you from me."

Suddenly, my jeans pool around my ankles, my panties with them, as I feared.

Josh pauses and just looks at me, his eyes appraising all of my exposed parts. I've never felt more vulnerable in my life.

Then his eyes return to my face.

"I don't want your first time to be on the ground in this living room—you should be in my bed."

Does he really expect me to just turn around and walk there?

"Not happening."

"Suit yourself," he says, and to my utter shock, he picks me up and starts walking me toward his bedroom.

I knew he was fit and had to be somewhat strong, but I had no clue he'd be able to pick my heavy ass up! He's not even struggling.

This new side of him is doing all sorts of things to me, and I'm definitely wet.

Still, I'll fight him till I can't fight him anymore.

I really don't want to lose my friend, no matter how much my horny cunt is screaming for him to fill me.

He lays me down on his soft bed, and as he climbs over me, I whimper, "Josh..."

"Give up, Janine, and get ready," he says before burying his face in my neck.

I arch my back as a jolt runs through me, and I can't believe how sensitive my neck feels. I can't take his lips there, sucking on my skin, kissing me on one side then the other.

I'm squirming and trying to push him away, but all he does in return is trail a finger down my bare abdomen, making me shudder at the thrill that runs through me.

Every part of me seems to have turned into raw nerves; every contact with my exposed skin makes me helplessly twitch.

Then his trailing finger reaches my pelvic area, and I tense even more.

Just when I thought things couldn't possibly get more unbearable, his hand reaches my pussy, and he lightly brushes a finger across it.

I lose it, twisting and turning against his touch, unable to do anything to help control my reaction to him, to calm the growing desire in me.

He's making me crazy, and I don't know how to handle myself—I've never felt anything like this before, and I'm not equipped to fight him in any way.

"Please," I beg as he fondles my pussy.

Very gently, he pushes part of his finger inside me, making me whimper some more.

"Oh, Jesus, Janine," he whispers.

He withdraws his finger and sucks it, then he replaces his finger with his mouth and my mind completely blanks.

No thought or words form—I've been sent to a place where I can't see or hear; I can only feel.

Eventually, after a few seconds or minutes or so, I realize I'm moaning desperately and grabbing his sheets while I twist against his warm, wet tongue lapping at my sensitive folds, getting me one step closer to begging him to take me to the finish however he wants to.

Then he stops and sheds his clothes completely, and I have no sense of time—just that he's naked before I can even register what he's up to since most of my mind is still in some stratosphere.

He climbs over my quivering body again, and I just know this is the moment, but he reaches behind me and unclasps my bra instead.

"I need to lick them," he says. "I want to see them bounce and jiggle as I fuck you."

His words turn me on more.

Where did this horny beast come from? When did my best friend suddenly get so fucking hot?

He flings my bra to the side and just stares at my boobs before reaching down and grabbing them. He lightly brushes against my nipples with his thumb, sending more jolts of pleasure through me.

His hands continue to explore my tender swells as he settles himself between my legs.

I finally chance a look downward to see what he's working with, and what I see frightens me.

His pale cock is large and hard, too thick to fit inside me, I think. How the hell is this supposed to work?

"Don't you worry," he says as if he read my mind, "I'll try to go easy on you for a bit."

He starts adjusting his body, aiming his fat cock at my pussy.

I brace myself, closing my eyes as if it might help.

I feel the smooth head of his dick at my slick virgin entrance, and by then, I'm desperate for him to go all the way.

But first he plays with me a bit, rubbing his tip over my tingling lips and teasing my opening, making me even more desperate.

Finally, he settles his body again and guides his fat cock to my tiny eager hole, and I feel the heaviness of his stiff, fleshy member as he pushes it in slowly.

"Oh god," he says as he makes headway.

I try to relax as he pushes further in, opening my legs more to help ease the pressure, but all I can feel is him—there's no alleviating the feel of his rock-hard dick parting my virginal walls.

"Jesus, Janine, I'm really trying," he says, and I don't

know what he's talking about, nor can I concentrate on much but the dull pain of his penetration.

"I don't want to hurt you, but…"

My eyes open as he stops suddenly.

Poised over me, his own eyes closed, I hear him taking deep breaths.

I take the time to admire his sinewy form: his arms bulging with muscles, his strong, defined chest, the washboard ripples of his abs.

Then I notice his thick white cock partially inside me, and the sight turns me on even more. But I also realize he's barely even halfway in, and I feel like I can't take any more.

I notice his breathing has slowed down, and he starts pushing his dick deeper inside me.

"Oh god, Josh," I whisper as he continues moving.

"Sh," he says, as if I'm throwing off his concentration.

Maybe I am. Maybe that's why his eyes are closed.

"Look at me," I say softly. He shakes his head, pausing again. "Why not?" I ask.

"Janine, if I get a load of your beautiful body beneath me right now, those gorgeous tits of yours staring at me, and your cute fucking face, I'm afraid I'll lose it and hurt you. You'll feel me for days anyway, but if I lose control, much longer than that."

He starts moving again, diving deeper.

Finally, it's like he hit a wall and stops again for a moment. Then he moves his cock inside me, lifting and lowering his hips so he's thrusting, gently plunging into my depths.

I'm grateful he's taking it easy on me because the pressure of his hard, long cock is shocking. Who knew he was packing like this?

I have nothing to compare it to, but I'm pretty sure his cock would be huge to anybody. It's no less than nine inches long, and that circumference—good lord, he could rip me if he moves any faster.

He lets out masculine groans, and they get to me, relaxing me a bit.

I grab on to him and bravely take his generous dick, glancing down every now and then to watch it disappear into my pussy, glistening with my juices.

I watch the way his abs tighten as he drills his cock into me, then lean back and relax into the ride once more.

At some point, I realize I'm moaning again, and his pace increases.

"Fuck," he says, then opens his eyes to stare at me.

I get lost in them briefly, forgetting everything else.

He keeps his eyes on me as he moves faster, and I gasp and call his name as his thrusts become more and more ruthless.

His head leans down, and his lips take mine, distracting me momentarily from his merciless cock. The kiss catches me off guard by its sweetness, its tenderness, making me relax a bit more.

The feel of his lips on mine, his warm tongue

exploring my mouth, makes me want to open myself up more to him. My body responds to this other intimacy with additional wetness, and he starts fucking me harder.

"Oh, Josh!" I cry, breaking the contact of our lips as the relentless pounding from his cock yanks me back to the reality of being fucked by him.

I glance down again—this time over his back to watch his ass cheeks squeeze hard as he thrusts into me. The way his butt clenches and unclenches is one of the hottest things I've ever seen.

"Janine," Josh says in a strange voice, one that almost sounds far away. It is a sound of torture, happiness, and pleading all at once.

I understand it as he digs into me, his pelvis smacking mine as he thrusts deeply and rhythmically a few more times. Then, with a shudder and a groan, he collapses on top of me.

I eventually realize he came inside me as unfamiliar warm liquid spreads in me.

"God, that was amazing," Josh says, panting hard. "And don't you worry—I'm not done with you yet."

He stays in place, his cock emptying inside me while his chest is against mine, and I can feel his rapid heartbeats. It moves me to wrap my arms around him while I wonder what the hell will become of us now.

I continue to hold him, listening to his breaths slowing down, enjoying the feel of his hard body against my much softer one, his dick shrinking in me.

Then it finally hits me what I've done.

I'm no longer a virgin!

My best friend popped my cherry, shoved his way past my hymen, and claimed my innocence. He will forever be the first guy I fucked, or who fucked me—I'm still not sure what to make of it.

When I think he has gone to sleep, I start to move with plans to get my clothes and sneak out of his place since I'm not ready to face him in the casual aftermath, but he stops me.

"I told you I'm not done with you yet," he says, then his lips find my neck again.

A tingling begins anew in my pussy at the contact, and while he kisses various parts of me—my forehead, my lips, my cheeks—I feel his dick getting firmer.

His hands begin moving all over my body, and after readjusting himself, he bends to capture one of my boobs in his mouth, working it even more than before. He sucks and licks, flicking his tongue over my most sensitive parts, then he does the same to the other breast.

I'm tingling a lot now due to his skillful tongue working my tits, and his cock is growing harder inside me. I'm about ready to go again, and as far as I can tell, so is he!

His hands continue roaming my body, and one finds its way under one of my butt cheeks.

He stops working my breast to plant another kiss on my lips, then he grabs my other butt cheek and starts moving inside me again, his hands firmly on my ass.

I lean my head back and happily accept him riding me again.

There's something different about it this time, and I don't know if it's because he grew inside me or what, but I adjust to him a little faster, and my body is even hungrier for more.

I slide my hands down his firm body until I'm cupping his butt cheeks too, and then I hold on for the ride as he plows me harder, his cock sliding in and out of me like he's giving me some kind of inner massage until I start to feel an entirely new sensation.

I suspect what it is, and as Josh leans down to nibble one of my ears, my body tingles even more—especially my yearning pussy.

I thrust against him as if that'll help calm this new craving.

As Josh grinds his body against mine while still gripping my ass, his masculine strength and command on display once more, I realize his vigorous passion is doing something to me too, aided by his thick cock exploring my depths.

"I'm taking you there, baby," he says as he gropes me some more, parts of him reaching out to other parts of me, my clit suddenly getting some attention.

The feeling I had earlier grows suddenly and takes over, and all I can do is lift my body toward his as he slams into me, his cock taking me to this new place, catapulting me into the stratosphere again. This time, I feel like I've actually lost my hearing, and I'm really seeing stars as my body explodes in climax.

I shudder against him and let the orgasm flow through me, vaguely aware of him moving faster and faster until he's coming inside me again.

4

———

JOSH

My mind is blown, and for more reasons than one.

Besides how amazing it feels to be inside of Janine and have her tight walls squeeze my throbbing cock, I'm blown away by how much I want to keep her.

I feel possessive of her beyond friendship—especially now that I've claimed her innocence—and having these feelings is new to me.

I'm also amazed I couldn't be bothered to pull out —there was no way I could do it; it felt too fucking good, and I'm floored by the implications of shooting my seed in her. She could be having my baby in about nine months!

Additionally, I'm blown away by how much warmer, softer, and overall better it feels to have her nude body against mine—much more amazing than I thought or fantasized or dreamt—and I didn't think that was possible.

She has wrapped her arms around me again as I lie on top of her—one of the most delicious feelings I've ever had—a feeling I could never get tired of.

"You came inside me again," she says.

I look at her face to see if the slight fear in her voice is reflected there.

Her eyes are a bit widened in fright, and I know I should calm her down before she starts to panic.

"It's okay," I say in a soft voice, as if trying to soothe a crying child. "You're safe with me. I'll be here for you, no matter what happens."

She keeps her eyes on me for a few seconds, then turns away.

I lie back down.

Before I know it, I've fallen asleep.

Janine is still there when I wake up, but she's out cold herself.

I slip from the bed to get some water, and I try to think of what to say to her, since I know she'll be somewhat shy and still frightened about what we've done.

She is no doubt feeling vulnerable now, and I need to reassure her again and keep reassuring her until she believes I'm not going anywhere.

It's been a while since either of us ate, so I order delivery then hop in the shower, reliving parts of our encounter during it, which makes me leave the bathroom with another woody.

I quickly towel off, wrapping the towel around my lower half, then I rush to check on her since I'm suddenly hit with the terrible fear she might've slipped out of my place undetected.

I'm relieved to see she's still there, sleeping like an angel.

I watch her for a few moments, enjoying the beautiful sight of her in my bed, wrapped in my sheets.

I know I'll be inside of her again before this day is over—I have to. I need to sink my cock into her warmth as often as she'll let me.

The heck am I saying? She didn't exactly *let me* the first time—she needed some convincing then, and I'll do it again and again, whenever I have to.

When she finally emerges from the bed, she immediately does what I eventually did: head for the shower.

I want to join her in there so badly, but she's probably pretty sore, and I wouldn't be able to resist taking her again. Besides, me joining her will probably shatter whatever courage she managed to build up in my absence to approach me about all this.

I'll leave her alone for now.

By the time she gets out, our dinner has been delivered.

I sort everything out on the table—the food, the napkins, the plastic cutlery, and chopsticks.

I guess she finally remembers most of her clothes are out here because she enters the living room with a towel wrapped around her, her bra straps visible underneath it—the only piece of clothing that made it to the bedroom.

"So," she begins with a shy smile, bravely making eye contact with me as she sits down in front of the table.

"So," I reply, staring at her, not letting her off the hook. I need some direction—I need her to say everything she wants to say, and I don't want to steer what gets talked about first.

"So you ordered us dinner," she continues.

Not exactly what I expected, but okay, Janine. Feel free to stall!

"Yeah, I figured you'd be hungry considering you came here over three hours ago and it's now seven o'clock—pretty much dinner time, regardless of when you ate last. I got your favorites—figured that would be cool."

"Yeah, of course. Thanks," she says, preparing to dig in.

I love how much of her legs I can see in that short-ass towel.

I notice she's avoiding eye contact with me again, and I figure I'll have to be the one to start the real conversation.

"So," I say, "no need to go out with Jermaine anymore, right?"

It's brief, but I catch a tiny smile at the corner of her mouth. It's gone in a flash, but I don't think I was seeing things.

"Guess not," she says dryly.

"What do you mean 'you guess?' You have no purpose for him. *I'm* here now."

She glances at me, one eyebrow rising sharply, then she turns back to the food.

I almost laugh, knowing if I hadn't fucked her, she would've had something snarky to say. But she's still a little humbled by her submission to me.

"So what are you saying? Are you offering to be my fuck buddy?"

"If that's how you want to put it, yeah."

"I don't know if I can be that casual about it."

"We don't have to be. I was trying to work within your own verbal terms."

"My terms included sex with a hot guy I didn't really know so I could move past it easier."

"I still think it's easier that you gave it up to me, Janine. Either way, I'm not going anywhere. I didn't hit it with the intent to quit it—that was never my plan."

She seems relieved.

"And what was your plan exactly?"

I grab her hands, accidentally knocking her fork out of it.

"I don't know, to be honest. It just involved getting closer to you."

She sits there in silence for a few moments.

She still doesn't look at me when she finally speaks.

"So here we are, closer than ever."

"Maybe even closer than that."

She finally looks up at me, and I practically hear her face say, "Huh? The hell are you talking about?"

"Point is," I answer her face, "I'm not going anywhere, and neither are you if I can help it. Yes, anytime you need an itch scratched, you know where to find me. But you can still find me here, available for everything else—Skyrim and beyond."

She looks away again.

It might take her a minute to get used to the idea, but I'm confident she'll take me up on all of my offers.

Besides, she seems to have already forgotten how this whole thing works, though she briefly brought it up herself—my little guys are already swimming their way up her body, and I will send them into her tight canal over and over again.

I know it's just been twice so far, but one time is all it takes for a seed to take root. And from the gleam I now see in Janine's eyes, the next time I get to shoot my cum in her will be very soon.

END

NOTE: *Claimed by You* is the final short story in the *Tied to Him: My BFF* series. If you want more sexy interracial tales, head on over to the *Alpha Second Chances* series where the stories are longer (novellas/short novels)!

UP NEXT: An excerpt from book 1 in the *Alpha Second Chances* series: *Fated* (A BWWM Billionaire & BBW Romance).

SYNOPSIS: Sweet, curvy Nina has been in love with her best friend, Brent, for years. She accepts being friend-zoned until one steamy, impulsive night changes everything between them. But then Brent suddenly vanishes from her life, leaving her alone, confused, and carrying around a huge secret. When she runs into Brent again, both of their lives have changed drastically, and now that her old best friend is a billionaire, she's convinced he'll never want her now that he can have any woman he desires, and especially once he finds out what she's been hiding for years. But will Brent surprise her after all? Or will he toss her aside again, leaving her alone and broken once more?

EXCERPT

FATED

CHAPTER ONE - NINA

The first time I ran into Brent Colton I was five years old.

I was rushing back to my kindergarten class, late from having wandered farther than usual over the course of the break, and I came across a tumble of action—obvious among the deserted grounds.

I realized three boys were beating the hell out of a smaller one crumpled on the ground, who was trying to fend off the blows with his tiny arms as he covered his head, his body curled in defense against the vicious attack.

The boys were older than me, and although I was a little chubby (a characteristic that stuck with me for a while), I was still much smaller than any of them, yet I charged toward that group like I had hidden judo skills and guardian angels, and yelled for them to leave him alone.

I knew nothing about the situation—whether their victim was guilty of anything or not—but what I saw didn't look right, and it sure as hell didn't look fair.

If it had been two guys fighting each other, I might not have intervened, but three against one?

I must've looked a sight, or maybe they didn't like having a witness; in any case, one boy got in one last kick before another tugged at his shirt and the three of them sped off.

I ran over and knelt by the crumpled boy.

"Are you okay?" I asked, despite the obvious.

I only got a grunt in return.

My eyes scanned him and the surrounding space.

His thick, dark hair was ruffled, his otherwise smooth, creamy face blotchy, his glasses askew, and the contents of his lunch box all over the place.

I started gathering them together while he slowly raised himself to a sitting position.

"Thanks," he said, looking sort of adorable with his glasses all slanted, leaving one blue eye free and the other trapped behind cracked glass.

He adjusted his spectacles as best as he could to sit properly on his face.

"I'm Brent," he said.

"I'm Nina," I said with a smile, trying to cheer him up. "Why were those guys beating on you?"

He shrugged. "Because they can," he said.

I helped him the rest of the way up.

Unsurprisingly, we became fast friends, and we stayed that way for two years—until my family moved from the area and I had to go to another school.

I later realized our move was due to my father losing his job and our lifestyle being downgraded.

I also learned later what a competitive private school I'd been enrolled in; my parents had tried to get me on the path to Ivy League and thought attending that special school would help, but I ended up in public school for the rest of elementary through high school, which brings me to the second time I ran into Brent.

The first week of freshman year of college I felt a little scared and a lot alone.

Brent and I hadn't stayed in touch, so I had no idea he'd be attending the same university as me until I saw him strolling toward me as I headed to the cafeteria.

We both sort of stared at each other for a while, slowing down our steps until we figured out about the same time that we knew each other.

"Nina?" he said wondrously, his beautiful blue eyes —sans glasses—widening a bit and a small smile beginning to spread on his face, almost dazzling me.

"Brent!" I squeaked with joy.

Jesus, the years had been good to him—he was a certified hunk.

I ran toward him, closing the distance between us in a hurry and we slammed into a tight hug.

At first, I'd been tickled by seeing a familiar face, and I was relieved it belonged to someone I felt I knew pretty well—someone who'd been my best friend at some point—but as Brent's hard, muscular body gripped mine, his strong arms enveloping my soft body, it began to sink in even more what the years had done to us.

We were a bit past the teenager stage, but still very young and hormonal, and very distinctly male and female.

My generous, pillowy breasts pressed against his hard chest, and other parts of us lining up sent awareness shooting through my body, raising my temperature astonishingly quickly.

I was still a virgin, but my usually quiet pussy suddenly got chatty, begging for more of what she got a hint of as our pelvises pressed against each other.

I pulled away, startled at the sudden animal lust taking over me.

I took a step back and examined Brent again—this time from up close.

He was well-built and handsome, and he looked a *lot* different without his glasses—so much so that it was a wonder I recognized him at all.

I suppose the general way he held himself tipped me off, helped by the way his blue eyes bore into mine when he realized he might know me.

Brent and I launched into a quick catch-up

conversation, filling in the years with places lived, schools attended, intended majors.

At some point, in the new deep voice I still couldn't get over, he said, "I can't tell you how happy I am to see you, Nina. Of all the college acceptances, I picked this one, and here you are. Looks like we're destined to be friends!"

I tried not to show how much my heart had fallen at his words and chastised myself for expecting anything else.

How could I think for a moment we could be anything more?

We'd been separated for ten years, and we'd only ever been friends way back then—what else was he supposed to say?

Plus, it was obvious that's all he'd ever see me as—I was still chubby and unremarkable-looking—no lustrous, eye-catching hair to offset my staggering plainness, no sassy beauty mark adding allure to my face or neck. *Of course* I was destined to be friend-zoned—how could he see me as anything but his chunky, brown-skinned friend?

But no matter how much reason I tried to talk into myself, I couldn't stop wanting more from him, more *of* him.

Where the hell had it come from?

Sure, he was a fine specimen, but I didn't know current Brent at all, despite having talked to him for a while as we reacquainted ourselves.

All I knew was that the sound of his new rich masculine tones had sunk into my memory, and I longed to hear him when he wasn't around.

We easily became good friends again, and this time, we had *way* more to talk about than games and toys.

We ended up having a few classes together, and Brent had trouble with one, in particular, so we spent quite a bit of time going over class material.

At the end of an all-nighter before a test, he thanked me and said, "You saved my ass again. How is it you always manage to rescue me—one way or another—whenever we run into each other?"

I didn't really know what to say to that so I just shrugged and smiled as I looked away, unable to take his eyes on me.

"You have a really pretty smile, you know," he said in a suddenly serious tone, and I felt myself blush furiously, my skin heating so much, I almost wanted to dunk my head in ice to prevent brain damage.

"Thanks," I mumbled, though I'm not sure it came out intelligible; the attention he was giving me at that moment was absolutely demolishing my faculties.

Sure, I'd had a small crush on him that crept up on me during our friendship as kids, but what I felt for him now seemed far more dangerous.

I was too invested in every look and smile he gave, too curious about what he looked like beneath his casual clothing.

The sight of his bicep jumping whenever he moved an arm deranged me, and it seemed like I couldn't stop my eyes from going to his lips.

I wanted to look after him in a way that was inappropriate for what we were—just friends.

To make things worse, I watched him change girlfriends every few months—all attractive, slim women who seemed nice enough and never threatened by me, of course. Why would they be?

That is, until one particular girl—Stacey.

"She thinks you're in love with me," Brent said lightly as we headed for the library one day—as if the notion was absolutely ridiculous—but his eyes searched my face for a reaction and response.

I didn't blame Stacey for being concerned about the time Brent and I spent together, but it's not like I'd embarrass myself and make a move on him; I was clearly not his type.

I forced a laugh and said, "What?" then changed the subject.

I know, I know—smooth.

I did the next best thing to make up for the fumble—once a classmate took interest in me, I started entertaining it.

It was nice to get some attention finally, and the guy wasn't bad-looking.

Plus, I didn't want to stay alone, longing for something I couldn't have.

What a loser I'd be if I kept pining after Brent,

right? Especially when it was clear as a Spring morning that beautiful Brent wasn't about to give me the time of day.

This big girl needed some love too.

I introduced my interested classmate to Brent one day, not really expecting anything, but a strange change came over my old friend's face.

Brent's eyes locked on the guy in a way that alerted something in me, but I couldn't figure out what was going on.

Everything else about the interaction was neutral —the greeting words chosen and his tone of voice— but it was as if Brent didn't blink the whole time the three of us shot the breeze.

Things took a definite turn after that.

My admirer backed off inexplicably, and when I finally worked up the courage to approach him and ask why he hadn't asked me to lunch again, he said the oddest thing, "Obviously, you're taken."

He shrugged, not meeting my eyes.

"Excuse me?" I said.

I'd almost said that I never even had a boyfriend, but phew! Dodged that embarrassment.

"Your friend, Brent," he emphasized, finally looking me in the eye. "Clearly, you're his property."

My body heated with anger.

I definitely resented this guy's choice of words, despite how much a part of me wanted them to be true.

I also wanted to confront Brent, but what was I supposed to say? It's not like I had solid evidence of relationship tampering.

Ultimately, I decided Brent had done me a favor—a guy as spineless as my classmate had no business being with me. Scared off by a glare? Come on, now.

I pushed him and his words from my mind, not daring to dignify his reasoning with further examination; after all, that dude was way off—no way Brent thought of me as *his*, not like that.

But when Brent called me over to his dorm just a few days later, my primal alarms started sounding; something was definitely off.

~

CHAPTER TWO - NINA

I'd been to Brent's room countless times: to pick him up before we headed to the cafeteria, to shoot the breeze, to work on a project or toss test questions around or whatever, so I had no reason to think this time would be different and I ignored my gut.

Once I stepped into his room, smiling at him in greeting, as usual, Brent pulled me to him with one arm while shutting and locking the door behind me with another, setting off my alarms again.

"What?" I said stupidly, unsure what had gotten into him.

Were we about to have a fight?

He looked sober and sort of steaming—almost like he was mad about something. I could practically see fumes coming off of him.

But before I could make sense of his actions or try to figure out what could be bothering him, his lips were suddenly on mine—blanking my mind of rational thought completely.

I had dreamt about those lips many times, fantasized about kissing them many more times, and now those warm, beautiful kissers were on me.

It felt electrical and intoxicating all at once, and my arms wrapped around his neck while our tongues danced with each other.

The heat between his hard body and my soft curves increased, and I felt a tingle travel down my body until it reached my center.

My pussy came to roaring life, wanting more as he pulled me closer and pressed his hardness against me.

I gasped a little in shock—had I done that to him?

I couldn't believe it. Where had all of this come from?

I didn't really care about the answers—only that Brent kept doing what he was doing to my lips and my body as his hands gripped and caressed it.

When I felt him working on his belt, reality suddenly set in.

Surely he didn't plan for us to...?

I reluctantly tore myself away from him, slightly

alarmed.

"Brent?" was all I could get out because my body began to betray me, overruling the tiny bit of sense that had momentarily returned to me.

We were both panting heavily, and watching my gorgeous best friend overtaken by desire kept mine churning, but what we were about to do was so wrong.

I'd been on the verge of trying to move on from my obsession with him, and he still had a girlfriend as far as I knew, so there was no way I was about to become *that* woman—the *other* woman.

"Brent, we can't," I said more firmly, impressing myself with the sturdiness of my voice, considering how I felt.

"I want you," he said huskily, his rumbling voice sending another sharp tingle from my ear to my hungry, wet core, and I began to lose the reasons I was protesting at all.

Here was the opportunity I'd dreamed about countless times laid out before me—the chance to get even closer to the man I was madly in love with.

What was my problem again?

Brent's jeans crumpled to the floor, and he started working on my top.

I was bereft of words but not thoughts as I realized he was about to see a whole lot more of me, my lady lumps bare to his eyes pretty soon.

Since my words had failed us, maybe the sight of my thick, toneless naked body would stop him, and he'd suddenly start pulling my top back down and his pants back up in disgust—he was used to chicks who could fit the clothes on mannequins, after all.

"You're beautiful," he said as if reading my thoughts, then he flung my top away, followed quickly by the toss of my sensible black bra, exposing my ample twin jugs.

"My god, you're a goddess," he said before bending to fill his mouth with one of my breasts.

My nipple hardened under his sweeping stimulation, his moist tongue flickering over my flesh as he sucked one breast and fondled the other.

My underwear was damp by then, and with Brent moving his mouth to my other breast while working on my jeans, I knew I was about to lose whatever moral battle I'd been fighting.

I was still self-conscious about my body, but my longing and desire outweighed it by far.

Soon, I was in a daze, a state of paralyzing disbelief. How could this possibly be real?

"Lie down," Brent suddenly said, indicating his bed with his eyes and a tilt of his chin. "On your back."

His commanding tone left no room for disobedience.

I tried not to think about his hungry blue eyes assessing my chunky backside now exposed to him as I headed for his bed and did as he said, my chest lifting and falling rapidly as fear, joy, and desire mingled in me.

Should I tell him I'm a virgin? Will that ruin everything? What if he has a 'no virgins' rule?

Then again, what if he thought I was just awful at the whole thing? If he knows it's my first time, he'll cut me some slack, right?

I stopped thinking once he worked his shirt off, and I gaped at his muscled torso and the tight, rippling abs leading my eyes down to his tented boxers.

Christ, it was all real.

His cock was hard, long, and ready, and in a few minutes or less, he'd be pushing it inside me.

He crawled over me and my fear grew stronger as the momentous occasion neared—fear of what engaging in this intimate act could mean for us.

If we made love to each other, there was no going back to the way things were.

I thought he would slip his dick inside me right away, but his lips sought mine again, and I found myself relaxing with his gentle kiss, my hands lifting to cup his head while we explored each other's mouths again.

Then his lips left mine to trail down my neck, and the sharp, tingling sensations kept up my distraction, making me twist and turn at the currents of electricity zipping through me.

My yearning pussy started begging for him, and I thrust as if to encourage him to get going and start plowing me.

But he kissed his way down my chest, holding on to

my generous boobs as his tongue and lips skimmed my eager, desperate flesh all the way down my stomach.

Then he started nibbling at my inner thighs.

"You're so wet," he said before his mouth clasped my pussy, and I arched and probably yelped my pleasure loudly. Whatever sound escaped me was definitely more than a moan, and I felt helpless to what he was doing to my body as he licked and pulled at my sensitive folds, his tongue darting between them and over them, and then making me almost lose my senses when it flickered over my hypersensitive clit.

I was a brainless mush by the time he raised himself back up and guided the smooth head of his thick, stiff cock to my dripping entrance.

Reason and logic still had a few points to make, but desire had them bound and gagged, and when Brent leaned forward a little as he started pushing his hard dick into my tiny, wet hole, everything but the need for more silenced.

"You're mine," Brent growled into my ear, his words almost distracting me from the sharp pain of his rigid penis forcing my tight walls apart while my heart soared.

Then he stopped moving, only partway in.

"Shit, you're so tight, Nina," he said. "Don't tell me you've never..." His face suddenly contorted as if something took over him, and he pushed deeper inside with more force.

I thought he was all the way in until I chanced a

glance downward and noticed he still had more to go.

I gritted my teeth against the ache deep inside me, and despite the discomfort, Brent's thick cock filling me felt right, and my slick, eager pussy was soon yearning for more.

"Don't stop," I begged, though I knew he wasn't going to.

Instead of jamming the rest of his dick in, he started sliding it in and out, and my body relaxed under the new sensation, appreciating the gentle cock massage.

Soon, I wanted him deeper, and I adjusted myself to wrap my legs around him and try to push him farther inside.

His pace increased, and his thrusts got deeper and deeper until our pelvises slammed against each other.

Pleasure overwhelmed me, and I matched his thrusts greedily, taking as much as I could get while still wanting more and more.

His cock fucking my needy pussy felt like the most natural thing in the world, and when he started moving even faster and more desperately, I instinctively knew he was close to the edge of orgasm.

Knowing he was about to come from the tight squeeze of my cunt on his engorged dick took me closer to the edge myself, and when his thumb suddenly touched my clit and started massaging the oversensitive nub, I lost all control.

As he slammed against me in his finishing thrusts,

I came loudly and unexpectedly, shocked by the initial paralyzing contraction and the pulsating aftershocks of my climax as he squeezed our bodies together with a final tightening of his firm ass as he came inside me, our bodies flooding each other with orgasmic juices.

I didn't think about what that could mean then—I couldn't think at all, still lost in the glittering emotions overtaking me—love, joy, and wonder.

Ecstasy.

Brent soon collapsed on top of me, and I relished the feel of our hearts beating hard and fast against our heated chests.

I wrapped my arms around him, feeling as if nothing could bring me down, grinning widely.

It took Brent long enough to come around, but there we were—college seniors soon to graduate, and we had finally taken an important leap forward in our relationship.

"I love you," I said, the words escaping me in a breathless whisper, coasting on unadulterated affection and bliss.

Brent stiffened, then said one of the worst things he could say—a phrase that never showed up in any of my fantasies after making love to him at last, "I'm sorry, Nina. That shouldn't have happened."

My heart didn't shatter exactly—it felt more like someone had shoved a knife through it and then tore a path upward.

The feeling seemed astoundingly literal, the

sudden searing chest pain leaving me speechless.

Brent couldn't have possibly meant those words—not after knowing how I felt about him and after taking what he had from me.

He couldn't possibly think he could just take it all back with an apology—that, with a snap of our fingers, it would be like it never happened. There's no way he figured things could ever be the same.

My throat started closing up, and I fought hard against the tears welling in my eyes, my mouth trembling with the effort, but I lost embarrassingly.

"Listen, this doesn't mean I won't see you again," he said, tucking some of my hair behind my ear. "We're friends—always been—and it seems we're destined to be, so I wouldn't worry about it."

If I hadn't been so wrapped up in pain, I probably would've kneed him in the balls.

Well, that's what I thought once sorrow gave way to anger—I don't know if I could have actually inflicted physical pain on him like that, no matter how much I wanted him to feel a smidgen of what he'd made me feel.

Which finally brings me to today.

About five years have passed since that delicious deflowering ended so unceremoniously, and right now, I'm heading back to work from my lunch break.

My car suddenly starts jerking, and I don't know what the hell's wrong with it this time, but the highway's not the best time for shit to happen.

My eyes go to the gas gauge and I see the needle's at the halfway mark, so I'm not out of gas.

I turn on the hazard lights and head to the right, hoping to make it to the shoulder safely.

Lucky for me, I get there without incident, and I try not to think about how late I'll probably be getting back to the school.

My eighth-graders probably won't be too mad, though.

I bought this car off of Craigslist four years ago, once I had finally secured consistent work and decided public transportation wasn't for me.

About seventy-five percent of my campus job earnings went toward my college fees to pay them off sooner than later, and then the expenses afterward...oh boy.

Money was tight, so I figured it was easier to pay a lump sum and buy an old car rather than come up with money down and monthly car payments over two to three years because as far as I had gathered, I could own a car for the price of that same money down plus just one or two of those monthly payments.

A better deal, I thought.

Ha!

Anyway, it's broad daylight, so I'm not too worried about leaving my car to check out the exterior and see if the problem is something obvious, like a flat tire.

I've had a few of those, and the jerking I felt could be a variation on that theme.

I never got a flat tire while on a highway—it was always after cutting through some alley or during a drive down a residential street—so perhaps the difference in speed accounted for the slight difference in feel.

I hop out and check the driver's side.

Both front and rear tires look fine, but I kick them anyway and they both hold firm.

I head to the other side as a gorgeous, sleek, expensive-looking black car zooms by, looking like it popped out of the future.

I peel my eyes away from the stunning vehicle to check my passenger's side tires, giving them the same treatment as the others.

Tires firm, more than enough gas—what the hell else could it be? Please, don't be the transmission.

Armed with a bit more information, I call AAA.

I'm not really surprised something went wrong again—this car has had to have something major fixed at least once a year since I bought it.

Usually, when I'm excited about having saved up a good chunk of money, not long afterward the car goes, *I'll take that now!* The next thing I know, the head gasket has blown or the brakes have failed (luckily, that one happened as I was pulling out of my parking spot, so with a panicked pull-up of the emergency brake, I didn't end up in a dangerous position).

Obviously, this car is on its last legs—it was already fifteen years old when I got it and had a hundred and fifty miles on it, and it's not exactly one of those reliable brands that you still see on the road here and there, thirty years old and still going strong.

I sit and wait for the towing service.

To my utter surprise, I realize the sexy black car I'd glimpsed earlier is now also in the emergency lane, backing up toward me.

My heart speeds up.

Part of me feels assured it's an expensive-looking car instead of a white van with tinted windows, but criminals could lurk in either, and who knows what kind of psycho could be hiding behind such a sparkly, opulent appearance?

I immediately lock all doors, making sure the windows are up all the way.

I dig around for the Mace I keep under the passenger's seat, and for good measure, I make sure the heavy flashlight I keep inside is also within grabbing distance.

I type 911 on my phone, ready to hit dial as the black sports car backs right up to my car, mere inches from the front of it.

Then, trying to calm the fear tearing wildly through me, I watch as the driver's door opens, and a leg covered in immaculate gray slacks and topped off by a shiny black shoe appears.

"You've got to be fucking kidding me," I breathe as the rest of the body emerges, and the tall, broad, well-suited form of Brent Colton walks toward me with twinkling blue eyes and a slight smile, straightening his suit jacket.

My heart pounds even harder.

A lot has happened since our graduation, which came about a month after our sexual encounter.

We didn't keep in touch at all; in fact, Brent's number soon changed and his social network pages eventually disappeared, so I had no way to reach him.

As far as I know, he and Stacey are probably still together, even though the few times I came across her on campus after we did the deed, she shot me such dirty looks that I just knew Brent told her about us.

I wonder how he painted our encounter? Did he make it seem like I was the aggressor? That I'd seduced him? Or did he come right out and say that we had been friends so long, he was curious and had to get it out of his system? Did he tell her that now that it was out of the way, he was one hundred percent devoted to her? Are they married now?

I glance at his hand and notice no ring.

I didn't really have a connection with any of his other friends, so I've been in the dark about his life.

Maybe now I'll get some answers to my questions; after all, now that we've crashed into each other again, there are some things I can no longer keep to myself.

Particularly the fact that he and I have a daughter...

Grab the rest of *Fated* from your favorite retailer!

ALSO BY ROWENA

Erotica Shorts

FORBIDDEN FRUIT: HIS BFF SERIES

TAKEN BY SURPRISE - Nicolette knows she shouldn't fantasize about her boyfriend's **sexy best friend**, Jacob, so she keeps her crush a secret until her boyfriend's troubles land him in jail, and Jacob makes it clear he wants her and intends to have her. Jacob can't stop the **dirty, lustful thoughts** he has of his best friend's girl, and now that he has a chance with the **young hottie**, he's going to take it—**hard.**

TAKEN FOR GRANTED - Avery's fiancé drains their financial resources, leaving them broke and depending on Chad, her fiancé's **hot best friend**. They have to find a way to pay **strong, muscular** Chad back for letting them stay in his condo until they get back on their feet, and Chad has a couple of **naughty ideas** how!

TAKEN BY STORM - Reese can't get **brown beauty, Eva,** off his mind. Unfortunately, she's his best friend's girl, but he can't stop the **dirty thoughts** he has of taking her **hard and unprotected**, filling her with his essence. He resigns to suffering the torture silently, but Eva surprises him with a friendly visit one day and ends up stranded in his place by a sudden storm. Now that he finally has the **delicious, nubile beauty** alone, he's going to give her far more than a piece of his dirty mind.

RAVISHED BY YOU - **Travis is overworked and under*laid*.** He returns from a military mission with a hunger greater than ever before, and is horrified when, instead of his best friend Joey, Joey's **gorgeous curvy girlfriend, Lisa,** shows up at the airport to take him home. He has secretly wanted to give it to Lisa **hard and raw** for years, and by a twist of fate, he now has a chance to turn all of his **filthy fantasies** into reality, **and he's about to take it.**

CONQUERED BY YOU - **Military man** Michael has finally figured out what **his best friend's hot girl** has been up to—flirting with him and messing with his head in various ways he thought were innocent at first, but eventually realizes weren't—the **sexy brown beauty** knew exactly what she was doing. Now that he's on to her, he'll take things a step further and make sure the tease thinks twice before she messes with a red-blooded man like him—and she'll learn her lesson **hard!**

AVENGED BY YOU - **Lonely Bridget** would love to get back at her ex and make him pay for how callously he dumped her. But she's not a vengeful person, so she simply tries to move on. Against her better judgment, she decides to attend a party thrown by her ex's best friend, Scott—**a sexy, muscular guy** she harbored a light attraction for but never thought of pursuing. But Scott has other plans for the dejected, no-longer-off-limits beauty, and he's determined to pull her out of the dumps and quench his own **burning secret desire** once and for all.

TRAPPED BY YOU - **Newlywed Tara** is already bored with her sex life and has some **naughty fantasies** about someone *way* off-limits—her husband's best friend, Tucker. She wants to talk to her hubby about mixing things up between the two of them with no intention of adding a third party, but her husband surprises her with her deepest, darkest wish: **his best friend taking her hard and raw.** Now that the forbidden fruit is no longer forbidden, things are suddenly shaken up far beyond carnal desires. Can Tara handle the changing group dynamics?

WRECKED BY YOU - Simone has been having **naughty thoughts** about one of her boyfriend's **insanely hot** military friends. She doesn't plan to act on them, despite the 'hall pass' she still has for her boyfriend's infidelity a few years ago, but when an opportunity presents itself to find out what it's like to be with the <u>huge</u> off-limits alpha male...well, she actually doesn't have much choice in the matter!

TRICKED BY YOU - **Sylvia is a *wanted* woman.** Not by the feds, but by just about every guy in her husband's circle—his closest friends. The military guys all try to hide how much they want to take her for a spin, but when the opportunity comes up, *friends* turn into opportunistic **fiends**, and Sylvia has no idea what she's in for once her husband lands the two of them in a mess his horny buddies are only too happy to bail them out of—on one **hard, raw** condition. Well, maybe two...

TAKEN FOR A RIDE - Cutie Cara thinks she's getting a chance to turn a **hot male friend** into a friend with 'hard' benefits. But a stunning betrayal delivers her into the arms of someone far less friendly—and a lot more dominant!

DEVOURED BY YOU - Sweet Ariana is desperate for some **oral action**, and her boyfriend refuses to give it to her. She gets him to consider it for **Valentine's Day**, but when Ariana discovers her boyfriend has been cheating, she decides to get what she wants from one of his **super hot military friends**! But curvy ebony Ariana gets far more than she bargained for...

Steamy Military & Mafia Romance
SCULPTOR
GUARDED
RESCUED
A NEW DON

Sexy Billionaire Romance
BOSSY
DARE
FAVOR
CONNED
CAUGHT

Naughty New Adult Romance
BOUND
PENALTY
STEP TROUBLE

ABOUT THE AUTHOR

Rowena Risqué writes steamy friends-to-lovers romance and erotica with an element of reluctance. She likes a bit of darkness involved as long as no one really gets hurt—at least, only in good ways. ;) Forced proximity and kidnapping romances are her favorites.

She enjoys making up circumstances in which two people are forced to confront their feelings—sexual and otherwise—to the object of their desire, feelings they've been hiding or running from because of a major barrier or conflict of interest. Usually, her characters have known each other for quite a while, so their first sexual encounter has been a long time...coming.

Rowena also writes outlaw romance novels starring strangers at odds getting to know each other better under the name Lexi Gold.

Contact:
author_rowena@yahoo.com
https://authorrowena.wordpress.com